ORIGINS
THE BLUE DRAGON SOCIETY

S. FAXON

NBBP

No Bad Books Press, LLC

ISBN: 978-1-955431-06-4

Ebook 978-1-955431-07-1

Edited by Theresa Halvorsen

Cover art by S. Faxon

In memory of Anne Rice, the true mother of vampires

CHAPTER I
ANTON

The moans of the dying sickened him. They'd taken to occupying the shadows of the homes they once lived in to protect their loved ones, but Anton knew it was only a matter of time until all of them were gone.

The symptoms of the plague started with oily, blood and puss-filled boils, then followed with a fever so great, it was thought you could cook an egg on an ill person's flesh. After that, no matter the offerings they made or the number of prayers they offered to their gods, the body soon crumbled and begged for death.

The long-beaked leather mask he wore irritated his porcelain skin and as far as Anton could tell, it didn't protect him from the sickness. Though the healers said the herbs stuffed inside the beak would help, Anton thought it a cruel joke that did nothing more than make his nose run.

Anton wondered, *Do we really have to endure the songs of the dying, while we wait for this to go away? Or are we waiting to start singing the same tune?*

His black boots could not carry him fast enough from the

filthy, death-lined cobblestone streets of his hometown and toward the comfort of his family's manor. The iron gates and stone walls of his home were finally in view. The facade of the house was the finest in town. Where all the others were drawn together with logs, Anton's home was made with iron and stone. With his father as the mayor of the town, Anton had only ever known a life of comfort and pleasure.

Anton's long stride turned into a run as he crossed the unkempt garden once so vibrant and alive.

And now it's dead. Like everything else.

Anton flung open the ornately carved door and slammed it behind him.

"How much longer will we have to endure this?" Anton hissed to the empty entryway of his home. He ripped the mask from his sweating face, slamming it down on the table in the hall. "Aida!" he shouted.

But the round-faced woman he'd known his whole life, the one who would drop everything to serve him, did not show. He stood, squinting in the silence a moment, listening for the sounds of her shuffling feet.

"*Ay-ee-da!*" Anton strutted into the main hall of his family's home, rubbing his cobalt blue eyes. The main hall, which once had been frequently visited by the highborns of their country Baradesh, was as still as a graveyard. Only his well-dressed father sat in his high-backed chair, staring into the fireplace. No other candles lit the room. A chill ran down Anton's spine. From the corner of his eyes, he saw shadows chasing each other across the walls and wooden floors.

"Aida! Where is that cow?" he demanded.

Instead of his servant emerging, his mother ran to him from the darkness and clutched onto his wrist.

"Would you *please* refrain from that shouting!" She kept

her grasp on him, her groomed nails digging into his skin. "What will the neighbors think?"

Anton leaned closer to her pale face and said, "Nothing. They're all *dead*."

His mother threw his wrist aside and turned her back on him.

Anton ran his fingers through his dark brown hair, which he pushed behind his ear.

That's right. It's always about them and never about me, is it, Mother?

"Where is Aida? I'm bloody starving." He headed toward the fire. Without the normal amount of candles burning or people bustling about this space, the many tapestries dangling from the walls of the home could not keep up with the drafts seeping through their manor's stone keep. Anton pulled his wolf-skin coat tighter over his shoulders, its fine white bristles tickling his unshaven jaw.

"Aida's dead," his mother said, her thin arms crossed over her chest. "Or close to someone who is."

"There's no one left?" Anton ventured, rolling his eyes. "So what will we do for food?"

She raised her shoulders.

This was laughable. "What? Are *you* going to cook?" Anton threw up his arms and dropped himself in the wooden seat next to his father.

"Where were you?" his father, Sire, growled, his long, graying beard hardly moving as he spoke.

Sire's deep voice made Anton gulp.

"On a walk." Anton's shoulders slumped like they would when he was a child.

"For *two* days?"

Anton's shoulders drew up toward his ears. "This house is

maddeningly dull and until your precious travel ban lifts, I can't -"

"We are in an epidemic!" Sire's white-knuckled fist slammed onto the wooden armrest.

Anton drew his arms in tight to his body for just a moment until frustration built up within him like fire. Gritting his teeth, he started, "*You* said that once the serfs died off, the gods would be satisfied and that we would be fine."

"Does *this* look fine?" Sire latched onto Anton's wrist and pulled the tunic from his own neck, revealing a large black boil.

Anton tried to leap back, sending his chair scraping across the stone floor, but his wrist was still tightly clutched in Sire's hand.

Sneering, Anton said, "You've doomed us!"

"No! Listen to me, boy," Sire shoved Anton's wrist away from him. "There is a healer in our neighboring village of Davensport. He *owes* me. Go to him, tell him that I've fallen ill with this. He has medicine he says can help, but he will not leave his store for fear of thieves. Go to him, boy. Collect the medicine and bring it straight back to me. Do not stop until you bring that medicine here. Do this, boy, or we're *all* dead."

Anton's lip curled. *Yes, father, I'll go to Davensport. But you've brought this upon yourself and I'll be damned if I bring this medicine back to you. Maybe I won't return at all.*

Sire hurled a goblet from the table beside him into the fire then shouted, "Go!"

Anton's knees buckled.

I'd have nothing without him. I have no choice but to come back to this hell.

Realizing he had no choice, Anton stormed past his mother, plucked his leather mask from the table, and shoved it back on his face.

THE SAWMILL WAS NOT MORE than an hour's walk outside of town. If their horses hadn't been stolen last week from brigands trying to escape their county and its plague, Anton could have crossed the distance in a half hour's time. However, the pouring rain turned the roads to mud, slowing Anton's progress. He hated that his nicest cloak was soaked and likely ruined, but what choice did he have? Though Anton was a man now at nineteen, the power of his father's fists and fury were nearly as much of a threat to him as this plague.

As he trod down the streets, he saw a cart with a horse ahead and two men wearing masks similar to his own.

His stomach tightened.

Even through the deluge, he could see the lumps of the dead in the wooden cart, their feet hanging off the end, some in shoes, some bare and filthy.

He gulped.

I will not succumb. I will not be carried out on a cart like rubbish.

Gathering the damp cloak around his shoulders in a fruitless attempt to stave off the cold, Anton turned down the thin alley not wanting to get any closer to the dead.

"Aann-tonnn."

He whipped around.

The voice had come from behind him, and yet, there was no one there. The alley was dark enough to where he might miss a person trying not to be seen, but not dark enough for them to disappear.

"Anton." The phantom voice was a whisper, but it penetrated through the hiss of the rain like a knife.

His eyes narrowed. Almost everyone he knew was gone and had been for weeks. Grunting, dismissing the idea of a ghost and rationalizing it as a product of his imagination, he resumed his trek out from this dirty part of town.

"Anton," the voice called again, once more from behind.

"Who's there?" he shouted, spinning back around. "Show yourself!"

No one. Searching the alley for a ghost felt like a total waste of whatever time he had left. "It's just the gods having a laugh while there's any of us left to worship them. After this bloody plague, why the hell should any of us bend a knee to them?" Anton sneered and continued down the alley. Just as he almost reached the end, a hooded figure stepped out before him.

Anton jumped back.

"Wh-who are you? What do you want?" His heart thundered in his head. How could the voice of this man have traveled all around him?

He has to be a wizard, he must be. If he's not...

The stranger, who looked to be about his father's age, stared out from beneath a hood. The details of his face were hidden by the darkness, and yet, Anton felt there was something not right about this being. Though a solid person stared at him, there was something off about his body. Like it was nothing more than a vessel being used for something other than life, something *far* darker.

"I'm warning you!" Anton's shaking voice threatened. "My father is a *very* powerful man. If anything happens to me-"

"Your father is dying, is he not, Anton?" the stranger asked his whispery voice cutting through the rain. "And why are you off to save him? Empower him once more to strike you with the back of his hand or the blunt of his sword? Or do you go to save your mother? The woman who ignored you your entire life except for when you *inconvenienced* her?"

Anton's heart pounded, his eyes wide. *How does he know this?*

6

"Do not be afraid of me, Anton. I have come to offer you a gift." The stranger's pale face barely moved as he spoke.

"Who are you?"

"My name is of no consequence. I know who you are. I know what you and your family have done to survive. I know what you could be."

Anton narrowed his gaze. "What do you mean?"

The stranger took a step toward Anton. "Two paths lie before you, Anton: you can continue on your father's quest to Davensport -"

"How do you-"

"You get the medicines, but what happens next? Maybe the little herbs will work *this* time, but what about the next time your father finds another boil? Or worse, when *you* find one?"

Anton's stomach felt sick.

There really is no escaping it, is there?

"There *is*, Anton."

"Can you hear my thoughts?" Anton tried to swallow, but his throat felt so dry. *Is he a god? Or...something else?*

The stranger lifted his chin slightly. "The *second* path will lead you to life."

"What? Are you claiming to have some sort of miracle drug? A potion that'll cure all our ails? C'mon. This has been going on for over a year. We've heard it all and your cheap tricks will not scare me into buying anything, sorcerer."

Anton started to turn around, but hollow laughter filled the alley, echoing from every direction.

"Go on then," the stranger continued. "Go die in your way. Say no to the gift of life. *True* life where you may live as you please and you'll never have to fear anything, even death."

Anton's boots stopped. He turned back toward the stranger.

So you are a demon then?

His eyes searched the being. He'd heard stories of demons his whole life. But he'd never actually encountered one, nor had anyone he knew. When he was a child, Aida had told him through her bedtime stories to never to make deals with demons. But the people in those tales asked for such petty things. This was a life or death situation; surely it had to be different.

Anton stepped toward the stranger. "What exactly are you offering me?"

The stranger said, "Simply that you come to the old mill where the Bull and Cedar rivers meet. I know you're a smart man, Anton. You don't have to agree to anything. Think about it. You can just walk away if you want, but, come see what I have to offer."

Anton held his breath.

The stranger shrugged as if bored with the conversation. "If you decide to come, be there at nightfall." The hooded man turned and headed out of the alleyway, disappearing in the rain.

This feels too good to be true.

CHAPTER 2
THE DEAL

The crumbling timbers of the abandoned fulling mill came into view.

This must be the place.

Anton's steps slowed as he crossed the bridge over the rushing tide of the Bull River. The fulling mill where once countless tons of wool had been cleansed over the course of decades looked about as desperate as the situation he found himself in. Several gaping holes looked out from the moss-coated thatch roof and not a soul moved around it.

Glancing back over his shoulder, Anton thought about the road to Davensport behind him, where the healer with the medicine was.

It's not too late yet. I could go there, get the medicine, and save my father, but then what? He'd still be a miserable arse. After all he's done, this plague is what he deserves. And if this tonic or whatever it is this stranger has to offer works and my father dies, I'll inherit the lordship over our little village and I'll be the master at last.

With a slight smile on his face, Anton continued toward the wooden front steps of the mill. Exhaling slowly, he said to the wind, "It's like the old man always said, to stay on top, you have to step on those below. And now, father, it seems like I'm about to rise while you fall."

The steps moaned and creaked as his boots crossed them. Anton raised his fist and banged on the wooden door.

A moment passed before the door opened a sliver. A pale face stared out at him.

Anton gulped, but he held his stance. *If it weren't so mysterious, I'd think I'd come to the wrong place.*

"I was asked to come here by a hooded man," he said.

The pale-faced stranger nodded once and opened the door.

Anton stepped down into the long hall of the mill. The scent of mildew and dust cut through the herbs of Anton's mask as he proceeded inside. He looked up to the exposed rafters overhead and saw nothing but shadows staring back. A small number of people stood scattered about the space, none speaking above a whisper. In the heart of the mill was a wide circle of flickering candles. Anton figured a full-grown man could lie in the center of the candles without his extended hands or feet meeting the wax. In between each candle were pewter goblets.

Strange.

The blinking glow illuminated the faces of some of the people, none of whom he knew, except...

"Riva!" Anton scurried by a few souls then reached out to a woman a few months younger than he that he'd known for years. When he pulled his mask off, her bright blue eyes doubled upon seeing him.

"I thought you were dead!" They said in unison.

"My parents and my sisters though..." Riva's high-cheeked face turned to the floor, tears filling her eyes. She swiped her cheeks. "Yours?"

Anton shrugged his shoulders.

She shook her head. "There's no one left. No families, no farmers or bakers, no one. Anton, do you think this is the end?"

Anton shrugged again. "What is all this? Do you know?"

Riva turned her tear-filled gaze away from Anton. "No. I was just about to...to give up when a man came to my door. He said he had a cure, a guaranteed protection from the plague. I was so desperate, I didn't know what else to do."

Anton nodded as she spoke.

"Do you think it's real?" she asked. "Can we trust this?"

"I don't think we have any options left."

A hooded figure emerged from the shadows and entered the realm of light. Though the hood still covered his face, Anton recognized him as the stranger from earlier. The man stood in the center of the candle halo and held his arms up. "Come, take a place around the circle and stand behind one of your chalices."

Anton peered around the circle. There were sixteen others all looking to be in their late teens or early twenties, like him and Riva.

Have you all lost your families? Or did you leave them to die like me?

The hooded man began, "Today, each of you were given a choice, to take your chances with the plague or to come here to take a leap of faith, a chance to be saved from the dangers our world has to offer." He touched his hand to his heart. "And you came. You know the risks you face out there and you were brave enough and smart enough to know that this is what is right."

He motioned toward the pewter chalices at their feet.

"This elixir will make you strong. It will protect you from any plague or natural force that seeks to destroy you."

Many of the people around the group exchanged glances.

Some looked intrigued, one or two looked hopeful, the others looked terrified.

Why be scared? Either it's poison and we all die now or it's real. That's it.

"I know your thoughts," the hooded man continued. "Who am I to be sharing this with you? Why trust me?" He bowed his head. "I seek to save this world from this plague that's destroying it. You are the ones who will emerge from this stronger. I know you've lost much, everything in some cases. But I promise you, together, we will rebuild, and we will come out of this as a family, forever bound together in this new life."

He raised a chalice that Anton thought he must have had hidden somehow in his robes.

"Together now, if you choose to drink it. Remember," he held a hand up. "You don't have to. No one is forcing you into this and you are welcome to leave, but if you stay, this *will* save you from the plague. You've all seen what's out there and I don't have to remind you how terrible dying from this plague is. That it tears you apart, consuming your flesh, torturing you with fever and pain." He pointed at the goblet. "But this will save you."

Across the room, one girl broke into tears. A young man tried to pull the crying girl closer, to convince her that this was what was right, but she shook her head and muttered, "I'm so sorry, I can't. You know what he is!" and then ran out from the mill.

The young man's shoulders drooped, his forehead dropped toward the floor.

"It's alright," the hooded man said. "I *know* this is a hard decision to trust someone you don't know. It's up to you."

The toe of Anton's boot tapped up and down. *Enough talk already. Let's get on with this.*

The hooded man raised his glass high as if toasting them

all, then set the goblet to his lips and drank. Once the man was done, he wiped his lip with the sleeve of his robe then said, "If you'd like, I'll do the same from any of your goblets to show you they're safe."

A number of the others exchanged glances, but Anton was done wasting time. He bent down, plucked his goblet from the floor, and drew it up. He started gulping the thick liquid down, undeterred by the metallic taste.

He felt the eyes of the others on him as the slimy substance rolled down his throat.

Anton finished the drink and threw down the goblet. The clank of the metal to the wood echoed in the mill. Anton wiped his mouth with the back of his hand and tossed his mask to the floor beside the goblet. He stared into the eyes of the hooded man, both now shining brightly at him from beneath his hood. At this angle and in this light, Anton realized that the man had no hair on his brows or head.

Anton looked to the people around him and motioned at their chalices saying, "What are you waiting for?"

The others exchanged more glances and some bent their knees to pick up their chalices. A few drank as quickly as he did, finishing their servings quicker than the rest.

In only a few minutes, they all finished, some looking green from what they drank.

"Very good." The hooded man nodded. "Now, we will stay in this mill for the night, and in the morning, we will move together to a new home in the mountains just west of here where we will build our community."

As he began to speak of this new collective, Anton's stomach began to rumble. It was soft at first, but then it turned to cramps.

Anton's hands clenched.

The fires of the candles blurred and the hard wooden floor swayed.

What's happening to me?

Sweat formed on his brow and ran down his cheeks. His stomach twisted as if the drink was trying to punch and claw its way out.

He heard someone say, "I don't feel right."

Anton gritted his teeth.

"What was in that?" said another.

Anton doubled over. The pain felt like a knife to his belly. He gasped for breath as his vision doubled.

"What did you do to us?" someone screamed.

Anton's knees hit the floor and the world blacked out around him.

CHAPTER 3
OWEN

Owen's black wings beat as fast as they could. With grace and power, he maneuvered his long, blue-scaled body around the pinnacles of the snow-capped evergreens jettisoning up from the mountain's peaks. Though many of his fellows back home thought him wild to be flying like this, Owen never felt more at peace than when he took to his wings. While his comrades felt content maintaining their human forms, Owen thought, *I'll never understand why they'd rather be humans when we are dragons.*

The legends of his kind told by the humans below talked of the castle atop the eastern-most mountains of Baradesh. The stories spoke of the dragons' stone castle carved and forged from the range, its towers rising high above the clouds. The scale of the keep was beyond anything created by man. No mortal had ever stepped foot on those stones, for the dangers of the mountains were too much for them to bear. The cold climb alone was enough to kill a man within an hour, but the warm blood and thick scales of the dragons protected their hides and made the freezing air of little bother. Without the disruptions of man, the Blue Dragon Kingdom was able to exist together in relative peace.

Owen sucked in a deep breath of the mountain's air. It filled his spirit and made him feel like he could soar across the entire continent within the space of an hour. He knew it was pointless to imagine such things with the restrictive rules of his kin, but a dragon of his size could reach the the thick banks of the Bull River, the snaking belt that split the country in half, in the span of a night from their home in the mountains.

Sure, he thought, *it's not the whole continent, but it should be far away enough from here.*

Dragons who had not yet taken their missions were only permitted to fly around their mountain range. While the mountains were spectacular, their scenery had become rather commonplace to Owen. For Owen, flying so low over the trees was the greatest thrill he could get while he waited for his trials.

If it means I don't have to actually go on a mission though, I think I'd be alright forever dodging the tops of trees.

A heavy pang grasped on to Owen's heart as the peaks of the slender, colossal black towers came into sight. Though he felt like he could keep flying for hours, he saw his father standing in human form at the edge of the runway where his kind landed. When Owen's father, Sten, waved his arm at him, Owen knew his flight time had come to an end.

Stars. What now?

As Owen approached, he prepared himself for his transformation. He pulled his wings back, extending forward the four talons of his back feet. He shut his eyes and focused on the spell his kind had long mastered. The painful transformation took but a few seconds. Owen's muscles tensed, stretched, and twisted as his body changed from dragon to man.

The proud, double-horned dragon became a man who

looked to be about seventeen just as his black-booted feet touched the snow-dusted runway. In this cold, Owen was grateful the spell always included the clothes and fur cape to protect his human body. Though his short brown hair, long face, and silver eyes were handsome, Owen detested being in human form. He took a moment before approaching his father to acclimate to not having a tail for balance or wing for flight. It felt so unnatural, especially the first few moments after the transition. However, the elders had long decided to remain in human form whenever possible for where a village of men considered a cow a feast, a single dragon considered a cow an appetizer. Saving resources for the mortals had become a priority while those below fought that ghastly plague.

Though his father's silver eyes were kind, the crinkled brow beneath his long dark hair told Owen something bad had happened.

"*Now* what do the elders think I did?" Owen asked, his shoulders drooping. He was so tired of being blamed for tricks the young hatchlings pulled.

Sten shook his head and adjusted the heavy furs draped over his shoulders. "No, Owen. It's nothing like that. The elders...they have a mission for you."

Owen wondered if falling off the cliff might hurt less than whatever they had planned for him. The Blue Dragons had long ago sworn to watch over the mortals, so every dragon when reaching adulthood took part in similar missions to aid humankind. However, after his mother's murder at the hand of humans, Owen knew they deserved every curse that came their way.

"You're one of the elders," Owen started. "Can't I have a pass?"

Sten shook his head. "No. Come. Go on ahead and talk to them in the hall and I'll go make the rest of your preparations."

Sten motioned toward the great castle across the landing strip from where they stood.

As they crossed the long runway toward the great hall, Owen kept his eyes locked on the western horizon. The icy breeze swept the powdery snow across the black stone. Owen's stomach felt ill as he watched the flecks of ice flying off over the cliff.

If only I could soar away and never come back like that snow. I'd find a way to never have to deal with man.

Beyond the landing strip and surrounding the castle was the log village the dragons long ago erected to accommodate their human forms. The town of ten, long buildings bustled with the fellow citizens of his kingdom going about their daily lives. Over the clatter of their activities, Owen could hear the metallic rhythmic beats of their smithy's hammer against whatever new project she was forging. Everyone in the village had a job to do or a role to play, except for the dozen or so hatchlings and Owen. Due to what happened to his mother, Owen's mission had been delayed to allow him the chance to mourn. While he understood the decision, Owen wished he could have just gotten it over with so he could finally be assigned a job in the village and have something to do. However, Owen often wondered, even if they did assign him a duty, would he be good at it? Would he really be happy? As much as he wanted to, Owen never truly felt like he had a place among his fellow dragons.

Maybe this mission'll change things. While it was a hopeful thought, with every step he took, Owen's wish to soar off into the horizon increased.

As Owen passed through the small market, he saw the stall nearest to the castle's wide opening displaying small baskets of apples and nuts. Owen's stomach growled at the sight of red and green apples glimmering in the afternoon sun. His mouth watered and he considered taking one, but there were so few in the basket. Food rationing had recently gone in effect to help the struggling people below. They were limited to one meal in the morning and one in the evening. Normally, this didn't bother Owen, but the flight he took to get away had left his stomach rumbling.

That's your own doing. Don't take an apple away from someone else.

As he passed the stand, something caught his eye. Tucked behind the cart against the wall of the castle, a single red apple shone against the snow. The cart keeper, bundled up in her furs, spoke with a customer on the other side, and had likely not noticed this stray. Owen bit his lip, looking between the apple and her back.

She would really never notice and it'd just rot if I leave it.

Owen reached from his path toward the apple, wrapping his extended fingers around it. The second he touched the cold skin, he knew what to do. Standing up straight, he turned back around and placed the apple back in the cart keeper's basket.

As he entered the hall alone, Owen saw the two elders gathered in the hall of their ancestors. The walls around stretched a hundred feet high and snow fell through the open windows onto the floor's slats of black stone. This palace was large enough to accommodate a crowd of dragons who could sit comfortably on their hinds without having to duck their heads. So seeing the human man and woman standing together looking so small in their surroundings was almost enough to make Owen laugh, but he knew better than to insult the elders like that.

Varden, a round-bellied man, stroked his long graying beard as he watched Owen approach. The other was a tall lean woman named Airell. Owen gulped when he saw her. From the short sword strapped to her belt to her glorious black hair that sat in braids on her head like a crown, Owen thought she always looked like a regal warrior. Whether in human or dragon form, whenever she caught Owen's eye, he felt like he was free-falling from the sky.

"Owen," Varden's deep voice boomed. "We have an urgent task for you."

Owen bowed his head. The feeling of free-falling from Airell's gaze suddenly felt more like being dropped into an abyss.

Varden continued, "In our efforts to help the humans combat the illness sweeping across Baradesh, we have found that it's not just the plague killing the mortals below. Some *new* creature has been born and they're living by sucking the very blood from the humans." The mist flowing out from his mouth as he spoke made Varden's words all the more chilling.

"Blood?" Owen felt his own life force draining from his face. "Are they demons?"

"Not sure how they could be anythin' else," Airell's velvet voice responded. Though she was the youngest of the three elders by several hundred years, she had proven herself worthy time and time again by both her wisdom and her might. "The sins of humankind have long let the lords of hell slip out from the gates meant to keep them at bay, but, thus far, nothing like this has ever emerged and, thank the stars, the king of the damned has never been set free. Despite that gift, demons are always the cause of anything going awry down there, but what purpose does this serve them? Just souls? It doesn't seem likely, if these...what're they being called again?"

"Vampires," Varden reminded. "The people are calling them vampires."

Airell nodded. "The vampires are wreaking havoc on the people of Baradesh. I searched the whole country over. I heard they're similar to the Rabeesa demons who make several slits in the flesh of man and then drink them dry, but these new monsters, well, they seem to only take a bite to bleed them.

"The people are terrified. They're speaking of end times, thinking this may actually be a plot from the king of the fallen himself to undo everything good."

The king of the fallen. Great. Please tell me my task doesn't involve taking on the head lord of hell.

Owen stood motionless while Varden looked down and shook his head. Though his tongue felt so dry he wasn't sure if he could actually speak, Owen asked, "So...what am I to do?"

Varden rubbed the end of his rounded nose then said, "Airell's done the preliminary scouting, but we need more information. Over the years, we have intervened on behalf of man when the threat of demons become too great for the mortals to handle. I feel in my gut that we'll be joining the fight soon enough, but before we do, we need to understand *why* the demons are doing this and what the weaknesses of the vampires are before we attack. We thought, after...well...after everything that's happened, this would be a good opportunity for you. You are to go down there, gather what information about vampires you can, and then report back to us. From there, we'll decide how to proceed. This will be a great lesson in patience and stealth, Owen. Do you understand?"

Owen gulped. Though he, like several generations of dragons before him, had studied the cultures, traditions, and religions of the mortals below, Owen felt like he was being thrown into something he was not prepared to face.

Airell took a step toward Owen and rested her hand on his shoulder. His knees felt weak as she said, "I know it's a lot, mate, but you're just scouting. It'll require little interaction with people. It's mostly just observation."

Varden nodded. "Once we have enough intel on the weaknesses, strengths, habits of these vampires, then we will know how to defeat them and how to send whatever demon is commanding them back to hell. Remember, lad, for the safety of us all, the humans must *never* know about us. Do not take your true form before them and *never* admit what you are. Just keep your head down and they won't come for you."

I'm sure you're talking about the vampires, but I'm more worried about the humans.

CHAPTER 4

PREPARATIONS

O wen spent the last hour in his small room staring off into the distance. The room was just big enough for the thin four-poster bed he sat upon. Though too young to recall the massive chambers the dragons once occupied in their dragon forms, Owen never felt comfortable in so tight a space.

A tear leaked down his face. He'd been trying to fight them back, but exhaustion wore him down. He snuffled then looked down at his hands. Nestled in his palm was a silver chained necklace his mother gave him two years ago. Rubbing his thumb over the oval pewter amulet depicting a rising sun, he recalled the conversation he had with his mother when she gave it to him.

"A necklace?" he'd asked. "But...we don't wear these. Varden says they're a symbol of oppression." He'd cringed at the time, recalling the stories Varden and some of his teachers had shared about the iron shackles mortals would place around dragon necks if ever they were caught in dragon form. While the spell they knew transformed their clothes, iron would not budge. Many a dragon

had been strangled mid-transformation in a desperate attempt to change from human to their natural state.

His mother though, her emerald eyes holding his, merely smiled and pointed at the sun imprinted in the amulet. "This necklace represents the eastern faith of many of the people of Baradesh. We look to the stars for guidance and they look to this."

Owen contemplated it a moment before saying, "The sun?"

"Yes," she nodded. "And what is the sun?"

Biting his thin lower lip, Owen ran his thumb over the wavy arms of the sun. "A star?"

His mother's bright smile had widened. She'd tucked her long, wavy hair behind her ear, then said, "Yes. See, they're not so different than us. We all look to the skies to find our way." She'd closed his fingers around the necklace. "One of them gave this to me last time I was down there and now I'm giving it to you."

Owen's brows raised.

"There will be times, Owen, when you'll be in darkness, unable to see the stars. Carry this with you so you know as they do, that the sun always rises."

Owen wiped a tear from his cheek. Though his mother had been gone over a year now, the ache in his chest was still as fresh as it had been when first they heard she fell.

"Son?"

Owen shot his eyes up and wiped his face. He stayed on the side of his bed but shoved the necklace into his breast pocket.

"I'm here," he said, his voice cracking.

Get it together.

Sten pushed the maroon sheet that covered the entryway into Owen's room to the side, entering Owen's quarters. Sten leaned upon the smooth stone wall beside the flickering torch on the wall. "I know this is hard, but our kind has aided man as helpful strangers for a thousand years. We protect them when things are dire, as they are now."

Owen bit his full lower lip. He stared into the fire beside his father. "I am honored to have been selected for this task, father, really, but I don't...I don't understand why we help the mortals. They're monsters."

Sten shook his head, his dark shoulder-length hair intermingling with the white furs on the coat he wore. "To many of them, in our true forms, *we* are monsters, which is why we must never reveal our true forms to them. Nor can they ever know where we live. Do you understand me?"

A knot tied itself in Owen's stomach. His fingers clutched onto the end of the furs he wore.

What you really mean is, don't make a mistake like mother did, don't you?

"Yes, I understand," Owen's heavy voice said.

Sten lightly tapped the ball of his fist to the wall then sat beside Owen on his bed. "I've instructed the messengers to prepare and send your provisions to your landing location. You'll be earning your first sword." Sten smiled softly. "I can't believe you're already ready for your trial. Seems like yesterday you were but a hatchling."

Owen rolled his eyes. "I'm not a hatchling anymore, Father. I've been flying for *years*."

Sten chuckled and said, "But you'll *always* be my son, Owen." Sten rubbed his neck then added, "Once you collect your sword and your supplies, you and your mentor will leave-"

"Wait, what?" Owen interrupted. He stood and spun toward his father. "A mentor? Father, I don't need -"

"You *do*, Owen." Sten shook his head. "I know you're smart, you're strong, your body has shown itself capable of healing as quickly as the rest of ours should anything happen to you down there, but...this mission...I can feel that you'll be grateful to have him with you."

Owen sent his eyes up to the top of his chamber. *I'm not a child anymore. When will anyone believe that?*

While gritting his teeth, Owen asked, "Who is it, then?"

"Lann."

Owen snorted. If it hadn't been his father sharing this news with him, he would have cursed. "Of *all* the dragons, why him?"

"Owen," Sten started. "Don't argue. The threat you face is unlike anything we've seen before."

"I am a *dragon* the same as he or anyone else for that matter. I'll blast my way through any force that thinks they can take me -"

"It is because of that arrogance that *I* have requested Lann to go with you."

It felt like his father had taken a knife to Owen's heart. *So it wasn't ol' Varden who suggested him. It was you. You don't think I can do this, do you?*

Sten looked away from his youngest son. "This is just a scouting mission. You are not to intervene, you are not to blast your way through anything. You understand? Stars, help Lann to be the calm to your storm."

Owen rolled his eyes. "More like the cloud over my sun."

"This is not about glory, Owen," Sten snapped. "The trials have never been about that."

"Then what are they? Airell did so well on her trials she became the youngest dragon accepted to the elders in an age! And Lann became a legend across the kingdoms from his. How can it not be about glory?"

Sten stood and placed his hands on Owen's shoulders. "Unlike the other dragons who have taken to the seas, to the rivers, or who have denounced the ways of man, our trials help us to understand balance. If you can walk among the mortals, you understand the balance of their world and ours. You appreciate how precious life is. That theirs are as valuable as ours."

Owen's stomach tightened.

But they don't see it the same way.

"What's more," Sten leaned closer to his son. "We're sure demons are involved in this, likely one that must be *very* powerful. We've all been trained with sending demons back to hell, but...son, *please*. Your brother has vast experience with demons from his missions. Please listen to him. Let him handle any demon attacks."

"Listen to him?" Owen raised his shoulders and slumped his head to the side. "Father, you cannot be serious? He's never even told me what he did on his trial. How am I supposed to listen to that cloud-headed-git?"

Sten shook his head and rubbed his eyes. "Owen, *please*."

"Fine," he growled.

I'll agree to whatever you want if it'll help me prove I'm not a child.

Sten pulled his son closer and kissed his forehead. "I know you and Lann don't get along, but if ever you're in doubt, seek his guidance. He is your brother and he loves you."

Right. I'm sure he'd love to see me fail at this.

CHAPTER 5
THE CEREMONY

"**A**re you ready?" Lann asked as he approached his brother on the landing strip.

Though only a hundred dragons showed up, it felt like the entire kingdom was present at the landing strip ready to watch Owen and Lann leave. A brilliant sunset illuminated the onlookers in their human forms, casting their long shadows toward where Owen stood.

At least they're too busy gawking at Lann to really notice me.

Turning to his silver eyed brother, Owen's shoulders tightened as he said, "Yeah. Are you?"

A bright smile illuminated Lann's clean shaven, long cheeks. "I am. This is your first time interacting with mortals, right?" Lann pursued.

Owen bit his lip. He was trying to commit to memory everything the elders reported to him about the situation, but Lann's questions were not helping him any.

You know I haven't interacted with them.

"They're really not so different from us," Lann continued. "Just follow my lead and-"

"Stop," Owen spun around. His brows lifted.

"Stop?"

"You're only supposed to intervene *if* I need your help."

Lann laughed then said, "Take a breath, Owen. I'm not going to overshadow your time down there. You're hardly the first to have a mentor go with you. Even father had one with him on his first mission. There's absolutely no reason to get your tail tied over it."

Don't let him get into your head. You won't need him. This is just a scouting mission. Don't let him ruin your special day. This ceremony is for you and now you'll get to prove to all of them you belong here.

Owen pushed past his brother and marched toward the center of the snow-covered runway where his father and the other two elders waited.

Maintaining his smile, Lann followed his brother, the furs on their backs billowing like waves in the wind, as they approached the members of their kingdom.

Owen pushed the air from his lungs. His fingers clutched around the necklace in his pocket.

This is it.

Once the brothers joined the elders, the mumbled voices of their fellow onlooking members ceased. All attention was focused on watching yet another one of their brothers begin their trial.

Owen concentrated on looking at Varden, ready to commence the brief ceremonies as he had for hundreds of dragons before.

Varden raised his fists into the air to draw whatever attention that wasn't already centered, to him. "Remember," the old dragon's voice rang out. "With the stars as your guides, you, Owen of the Blue Dragon Kingdom, are about to take part in a mission that our brothers and sisters have performed for over a thousand years. We go to the lands of humankind to serve as guardians when they are in need. You may intervene as you see fit as a dragon or man, but you must *not* reveal what you are to the people, and nor may you reveal the location of our home for the sake of our kingdom. Demons may hunt you for your soul and your blood, man for your scales, but no matter what, you will never betray this vow you make before your kin. Do you so swear it, Owen of the Blue Dragons?"

The elder motioned toward the sacred stone, a pointed block of obsidian as tall as a man, standing at the start of the runway. Owen made his approach. He shut his eyes and focused on the transition. He twitched and groaned as his flesh and muscles morphed from man to dragon. Stretching one's bones and turning flesh from skin to ocean blue-colored scales was far more painful than the other way around, but he internalized the brunt of the pain as he'd been taught. Before them now stood their black-winged brother, towering above them all. Owen extended his talons toward the stone and took it in his grasp. It now seemed so small in his claws.

Owen's voice boomed out from his dragon's teeth, "I so swear to protect my kingdom and my kind through the bond of silence. If I break this, if I reveal what I am or where my family lives, I swear upon this stone that I will never return home."

He flicked his wrist, spilling his blood upon the stone, mixing with the seals of countless dragons before him.

Twisting his long neck, Owen turned his gaze behind him. He saw the elders, including his father looking proud but worried.

If only Mother could be here. She believed in me.

"Go now," Varden said. "And may the stars guide you."

Leaning back, Owen released a long exhale. He turned his gaze toward the end of the runway and began his run. His feet and hands pounded against the stones as his bat-like wings began to flap. While taking off from a standstill with the power of their wings was more than possible, it was part of the tradition of the missions for the dragons to make this leap from their home and into the clouds. The edge of the runway neared and Owen's feet barely touched the ground. Reaching the end he pushed up with all of his might and took flight, his wings cutting through the air.

The mist kissed his cheeks, neck, and scales as he began his journey toward the lands of humankind. Though the shouts and cheers of his fellows echoed behind him, Owen focused on the prayer in his heart, *Though I don't want to help them, I won't let you down, Mother, I promise.*

CHAPTER 6
IN THE LAND OF MAN

Though he heard Lann's wings behind him, Owen did his best to separate himself from Lann. They'd been flying for hours. His wings pounded the night skies, slicing through the mist, drawing himself closer and closer toward their intended destination. Every now and then he'd glance back to see if his brother was really following him or if it had been some sort of joke and he was really being accompanied by Airell.

But no. Lann's black wings remained visible, the expression framed by his horns and spikes still content as ever.

Why couldn't Airell have come instead? I mean, sure, she makes me so nervous, I can barely talk, but Lann's an idiot with a big heart and he's probably going to get us both killed or worse, banned.

Glancing up to the map of the heavens, Owen saw by the twinkling stars that they were almost ready to descend. Though finding landmarks through the clouds below them was almost impossible, for Owen, flying beneath the stars was like curling up beneath a warm blanket.

But the growing cloud cover made it increasingly difficult

to align with the point of the constellations and find the field concealing their supplies. Owen glanced ahead. The clouds were far thinner, but he still could not see the bright glimmering star of the constellation he was supposed to align with.

Where is that star?

A great shadow passed over him.

Owen's heart jumped, but then his lip curled.

Lann was banking toward the north; he'd clearly found the star before Owen and was descending toward their mark.

Owen clenched his talons then double-checked the heavens.

Maybe he's testing me.

It only took a moment before he saw that it wasn't a test. Lann had found their waypoint and was already almost to the field.

Looks like I'm off to a great start.

Narrowing his wings, Owen raced toward the area, trying to conjure a story of making such a wide bank to ensure the coast was clear.

Yeah, that'll do it. You didn't do that, did you, Lann? Rather reckless of you, mate.

By the time Owen's back feet extended toward the earth, Lann was already in his human form, leaning against the tall stump of a fallen tree. Owen's feet thumped on the soft earth. He'd only ever landed in soft snow on mountain tops or upon the solid runway of their home. His feet stumbled in the soft dirt and his right elbow collapsed.

Stars!

His shoulder hit the earth and his wings tucked in tight against his sides just before he rolled. The peaks of the trees around the field spun up and down and up and down, as he tumbled before he came to a stop.

With labored breaths, he peered through the dust cloud around him at the upside-down line of the trees before him.

Has anyone else before me had a worse start?

He rolled over onto his stomach and reared back to get a look at where they were. The forest that surrounded them was dense and the sky above clear. He poked his nose into the air, trying to learn what he could.

In the corner of his eye, he could see Lann approaching at a casual gait, his hands tucked into his fur cloak.

Stars. Please, Lann, don't say anything smart about my landing.

Owen returned to his feet and shut his eyes, concentrating on the transition. The spell his kind summoned was not one they ever spoke. It was sacred and taught through touch. He recalled his father lying his massive hand upon his heart when he was but a hatchling, which, though a hundred years ago, still felt like yesterday. The power flowing through his core then felt just as special as it did today. Though he despised the mortals, having this ability that was passed to him by his father was the greatest gift.

Lann stood nearby watching Owen. Though he knew Lann was concentrating on keeping an eye out as they were never more vulnerable than during their transition, Lann's silence was proving to be just as annoying as his speaking.

Well, at least he hasn't made any jokes about my tumble.

Once he finished, Owen stretched his neck to the left and to the right, shaking his hands as he did.

"Now remember," Lann started. "While we're still strong in our human forms, our flesh and muscle are just as vulnerable as theirs. We'll heal, but it'll hurt, so let's just try to be as careful as we can while we're down here."

Owen nodded. "Right then, our provisions should be stashed in a hollowed tree near here." Owen pulled his coat closer over his shoulders and headed off toward the surrounding line of trees.

A full moon beamed above. Owen looked up into its eye.

"That's a great omen, you know," Lann said, pointing up to the moon. "It means our ancestors are watching over you."

"I know what it means." Owen tried to walk faster than his brother, but Lann's long legs kept up. He knew the moon should comfort him, but the sight of it made Owen's hairline sweat.

It means they'll see if I mess up.

It didn't take the pair long to follow their noses to the correct tree. The strong scent of the surrounding redwoods and cedars did not obscure the smell of pines from their kingdom or the delicious smell of smoked meat. Owen's stomach growled. Reaching into the hollow of the redwood's wide trunk, Owen felt for the leather sack. He stretched his arm as far back as he could, the hollow swallowing him up to his shoulder, until at last, his fingers found it. As Owen pulled the heavy, lumpy bundle out, Lann asked, "Excited for your first sword?"

Owen wasn't sure. A dragon received their first sword as a mark of their first mission. With every mission a dragon successfully completed, they were gifted a finer and more elegant blade or handle. While it was an honor, Owen was hesitant to reach into the bag.

I've trained with these for years, but...somehow receiving my own seems wrong. A sword is a weapon humans use against us.

Owen untied the leather rope and then reached in, pulling out the first item. It was a hefty cloth bag filled with smoked and salted meats. His heart ached. Because of the plague killing the humans, the dragons had sworn to fast to preserve the resources for the remaining people below. The fact that they spared this much food for them in human form made his heart ache.

Lann's hand fell on his shoulder. "We need the food to keep up our strength for the mission. The elders know that. We fast at home so those left down here will have more opportunity to eat and keep up their own strength."

That doesn't make me feel any better.

Owen put the satchel on the ground and reached back into the bag. The cold, metal touch of the pommel told Owen that this was Lann's sword. His fingers wrapped around the silver-plated handle and pulled the short sword from the bag. Owen's eyes widened as he looked at the embossed dragon, her wings spread and body curled in a circle within its brass pommel.

"Here," Owen said flatly as he handed the sword to Lann. Lann took the sword and pulled it from its equally ornate sheath. Owen tried to ignore his brother's examination of the blade as he tested its sharpness by rubbing its double-edged tip up and down one of his nails.

Right. Let's see what our ol' smithy gave to me.

Owen reached in and found the wooden handle. His shoulders drooped as he pulled his short sword from the bag. A birch pommel and handle proceeded the plain leather sheath. "Do you s'pose there's actually a blade in there or just a stick?"

Lann chuckled. "C'mon, you know we all start with a plain sword. And our smithy wouldn't dare give you a stick. You better believe that blade is sharp. She has her reputation to maintain, after all."

Owen pulled the blade from its sheath. The shining steel reflected the moon's light into his eyes. He tried not to wonder if the silver of a blade was the last sight his mother saw before she died. Clearing his throat, Owen mimicked his brother and checked the sharpness of the blade. It shaved his nail as if it was wax on a candle.

"See?" Lann started. "As sharp as the fins on our tails."

"Maybe sharper." Owen felt a bit relieved that his blade was at least as nice as his brother's. "How many missions have you done now?"

Owen continued to search the bag as Lann answered, "A dozen? Maybe more. And every one is different, though it has felt like we've been dealing with demons more and more recently. Maybe with the plague, the peoples' resistance to the temptations of the demons has waned. I know it's not a part of your mission, but maybe we can try to remind those we talk to about the dire importance of resisting demons."

Owen examined the leather straps he'd pulled from the bags.

What is this?

"Oh, good," Lann started. "Those are how we'll conceal our swords. They fit over our shoulders and, because our blades are short, we can hide them beneath our cloaks."

"Why would we need to hide them?" Owen asked.

Lann motioned Owen to stand. "Because," Lann explained as he pulled the straps over Owen's shoulders and settled the sheath in it. "We don't want to draw any more attention to ourselves than necessary. Our swords were forged by a master smithy by *our* standards. If anyone who knew anything about weapons or forging saw the quality of our blades...well, it's just easier if we don't have to explain or risk exposure."

Owen nodded. *That makes sense.*

"To get to your sword," Lann said adjusting Owen's straps to ensure they fit snugly. "You just reach back through your collar and the pommel'll be right there."

Owen followed instructions and found the pommel just below his shoulder line. "You really can't see it behind me?"

Lann shrugged. "Our cloaks are full. They'll be concealed, which is one more way that we'll be safe from detection." He picked up the satchel and pulled it over the top of his cloak. "And now, we are travelers. What next?"

Owen picked up the bag and shoved it back in the tree. "According to Airell, we should head that way," Owen pointed west. He shot a second glance up to the stars just to be sure. "She said the home of the vampires is in the mountains just to the west of us. And that there're some villages by the Bull River we should go to, see what the people there are saying 'bout the vampires." Owen gulped at the thought of having to deal with the humans, but he knew he couldn't complete this mission without talking to them. "We'll head that way for a few hours and then rest in the cover of the woods. Varden wants us just to observe the vampires, so we'll scout out from afar first then narrow in." Owen stopped himself just shy from turning his last sentence into a question.

"Sounds good," Lann said, as if sensing Owen's doubt in his plan.

"I wasn't asking for your approval," Owen snapped. He felt a foreign rage building inside him. It reminded him of the feeling he'd get before billowing fire. He rubbed his neck, feeling bad for snapping, but also wishing to get this over with quickly and go home.

Lann smiled. Owen's stomach sank.

You look so much like mother.

Lann shrugged then said, "There's no need to be so sensitive, Owen. I'm only here to help."

Owen rolled his eyes then began to trudge off through the forest. As they started through a grove of cedar trees, his mind began to focus on the ill-feeling in his stomach.

Do I really want to go home where they think of me as a hatchling? Maybe there's something I can do here that'll prove to them that I am a dragon worthy of their respect.

CHAPTER 7
GREATERS

H is tongue ran up her neck, pushing her blood to gush from the holes he'd made.

There was an art to drinking blood from his victims requiring grace and form, patience and skill, an appreciation that Anton had taken much of the last year to develop. It was so much more than just biting and sucking. This one beneath him, trembling and moaning from the touch of his fangs to her throat was more delicious than any wine he'd ever consumed back when he was mortal.

His eyes rolled back.

Supping from another brought him far more pleasure than any other act.

With a final thrust, he pulled away and looked into her eyes.

She, like many before, had been a gift to Anton and a great one at that. She'd kept quite well over the last few weeks, much better than the other gifts. The girl was so high on the opium he fed her that she had no idea she was about to die.

What a beautiful way to part.

The opium drunk through their victim's blood had thus far proven to have little residual effect on the vampires, giving them a considerable feeling of euphoria with none of the issues of addiction the mortals received. The taste of other luxuries, such as wine and food was greater now than they ever had been before, but there was nothing they craved more or needed as much as the taste of blood. *That* was their addiction as well as their life force.

Anton kissed her lips, leaving them red from her own blood. The beautiful ink glowed against her pale skin.

"Good night," he whispered as the light faded from her eyes.

He stared at her a moment more, holding his hand on her chest, feeling her heart slow. It intoxicated him.

He swiped a finger across her lips and drew a red circle on her chest. He bent his face forward and erased his drawing with his tongue.

Beneath his hand, her heart made its last beats, her final breath slipping from her lips.

"All good things must come to an end." Anton stood from his four-post bed and extended his arms.

A male servant jumped forward and draped clothes over Anton's shoulders. Though he continued to stare at his latest piece of art, Anton watched the lesser from the corner of his eyes. Lessers were vampires, the same as him, but they were newly born and had to earn their way out of their servitude. As the lesser continued to help him dress, Anton could feel how much the lesser hated him, despised him for what he was or what he had, whichever it was, Anton did not care.

Anton snatched the lesser's neck, and drew him to his face, dangling the man a foot off the ground. While the lesser grasped at Anton's wrists, Anton almost laughed. "I'm so sorry, Lesser, is there something on your mind?"

The lesser shook his head as best he could in Anton's clutch.

Anton clicked his tongue. For a moment, he considered ripping the lesser's throat out to show him how dominant he was, but Anton knew better and his belly was already full.

Anton pulled the lesser closer to him, their noses almost touching. He could feel the lesser trembling in his grasp. "No? Nothing to say? That's right. *You* are a lesser and I am a greater. You understand your place and don't you dare carry a single ill-thought against me. Do you understand?"

The lesser squeaked out a yes.

"Good." Anton threw the lesser atop the bed, tossing him with as little effort as a person would use to dismiss a fly.

The lesser bounced over the woman's body. He frantically whipped himself around and perched up like a dog caught in a crime.

And what will you do? So starved and confronted with blood? Would you actually dare to take a taste from the dead?

The lesser was visibly shaking, staring at the blood remaining on the woman's lips. Anton knew the lesser could smell it, that her still-warm body was screaming at him to feed.

"Thank you, sir," the lesser's voice quivered as he scooted himself off the bed.

Damn. What control you have. Pity. I would have liked to have torn you apart. I could use the exercise.

"That'll be all then, send for someone to get it out of here." Anton pointed at the body and began to leave the grand, windowless room. "Oh, and, Lesser," he stopped, looking at himself in the mirror, adjusting his fitted high collar to his liking.

The lesser stood straight as a board as he awaited Anton's words.

"Don't forget, one wrong move and you'll end up in the arena or worse..." He licked his lips and pointed at the girl.

The lesser nodded, his heart beating so loud, Anton thought he might dance to it. He sneered and continued on his way.

The shadow lord awaited.

THE ARENA ENTOMBED within the mountain reeked of stale blood and human waste. The one-hundred-meter-long sand pitch was a graveyard, littered with the bones and decay of the lessers and mortals the shadow lord commanded to compete against the armored mountain troll he kept. Thus far, only the troll had won.

Anton smirked as he looked around the tiered seats in the arena. It was large enough to host five thousand onlookers, but their numbers barely boasted a thousand as of yet. On occasion, the shadow walkers and the shy, hideous, blood-sucking Rabeesa would join them in the arena, though only at the bidding of their shared master.

The stone-floored pathway Anton tread on looked down upon the current spectacle. His lord's eyes rested on two lessers in the arena, the huge-bodied troll barreling toward them. The roaring brazier that sat in the middle of the egg-shaped pitch illuminated the spikes on the leather armor the troll wore. Anton recalled the day when he suggested the troll's outfit to the shadow lord after they almost lost their troll.

This way, he had said, *it'll ensure that only lessers end up dead.*

Catching the blasted troll had been terribly difficult, and not something Anton ever intended to do again.

"Ah, my prince," the shadow lord's voice hissed as Anton approached the raised platform overlooking the arena.

Anton tore his eyes away from a lesser diving to avoid a swing of the troll's bat. The crowd of vampires in the stands reacted with jeers and laughter.

They're only grateful that they're not the ones down there.

"My lord." Anton kneeled, bowing his head before the ornately carved throne of his master.

The shadow lord extended his clawed hand to Anton. Anton drew the demon's fingers to his lips and kissed the lord's knuckles.

"I take it you enjoyed your gift?" The lord did not look away from the fight below. The lesser still on his feet hurled a stone at the back of the troll. The troll spun around, swiping the lesser from his feet with his bat. The impact made a sickening crunch right before the lesser went flying across the arena, slamming against the center brazier. Bright embers flew up from the fire and settled atop the now motionless being.

Above the cheers of his fellow greaters in the crowd Anton said, "I enjoy everything you give me, my lord." He stood.

The hooded figure chuckled. "I know. That's why you stand where you are now and not down there in the pit. No, I sensed you were special from the start. You knew what I was back in that alley when we first met and yet." The pale face turned up to him and smiled, his red irises glowing out from beneath the hood. "You still came to me. When the others awoke from their transition, they balked. They were disgusted by the gift I laid before them in our home." He motioned toward the floor of the arena where Anton and the others had awoken with the lovely gift ready to be supped before them. "But you..." He sighed and leaned back in his throne. "You knew what you had to do and you did it."

A soft smile spread on Anton's face. He would never forget awakening face down in the dust of that arena, naked and starving. There in the center, spread out on a table lined with a white satin cloth was the most beautiful meal he'd ever seen. Though trembling from how weak he'd felt, Anton had used his hands and knees to reach the table. It took all of his might to reach up to the wooden table, to pull himself up to his feast to stare upon her. A halo of red hair surrounded the mortal woman's pale face and terror-filled, widened hazel eyes. Anton could feel the heavy pulsations of her heart, pumping her blood through her pale, naked limbs. His throat was the driest it had ever been in his life.

Using the table as a crutch, he made his way to her side. The craving for her metallic tasting wine was so strong, it controlled his every movement. Anton ignored the tears running down from her eyes as his locked onto the rapid rising and falling of her chest.

"You crawled to her, you *actually* crawled," the lord said like a proud father admiring the progress of his child.

As Anton's hunger had filled him with desire, she screamed for him to help her. Her plea, her limbs straining against her leather restraints, were so beautiful to him. It was like nothing he had ever seen before, but the growing instinct within told him exactly what to do with her.

Anton dove his mouth down to her throat and bit. Her scream in his ear had been nearly deafening, but the blood flooding into his mouth was the best thing he had ever tasted. His eyes rolled as he pulled mouth after mouthful of her wine into his gullet. She had squirmed and squealed like a pig being slaughtered, while Anton drunk to his delight.

"And when you were finished with her, you looked up to me." The lord shook his head and shut his eyes. "I can so *vividly* remember the blood running down your pretty face." He opened his eyes and caressed Anton's cheek. "I knew then. I knew that you would be my prince."

"I owe you everything, my lord," Anton swore. "Everything."

The pair looked away from one another just in time to see the troll rip the head off the lesser he had thrown against the brazier. Blood rained upon the fire and the crowd made a collected sound of shock that turned into cheers and chants, celebrating the troll's success.

The shadow lord smiled as he watched the troll take a bite out of the head in his hand. The troll's sharp fangs crunched into the skull as easily as a mortal would through the crust of bread.

Returning his gaze to Anton, the shadow lord said, "Your fealty is not one I will ever doubt, my Anton, but..." A dark heaviness filled the space around them. The light that had been in the demon's eyes faded. "I sense something and it troubles me. I'm not sure exactly what it is yet, but I know that it comes to harm us and everything we have done."

Anton watched the remaining lesser in the arena take to his feet and bolt toward the arched gate on the far side of the arena. The troll was too caught up in eating to notice, crouching over the blood-soaked body of the fallen lesser.

"What would you like me to do?" Anton asked, keeping his eye on the runner.

The shadow lord laughed. "That's my boy. Why not go for a stroll? Check-in on our Riva to see what she's reaping. I haven't heard from her in some time. Make sure she is still with us. Unlike you, Anton, I fear she may be drifting. Go and remind her *who* she serves. But, remember, we do not kill greaters. Bring her back to me if your reminder does not settle in."

Anton nodded. He kneeled and took the lord's hand. "It will be done, my lord." He kissed the demon's knuckles once more, adding a flick of his tongue to the demon's hand.

A bear-like roar erupted from the arena; the troll's declaration of victory. However, its cry drew Anton's attention back to the lesser on the other side of the arena. The man was crouched down and still as if focusing on something within him.

Oh, no you don't.

Anton placed the sole of his leather boot atop the rail that separated his lord's observation booth from the arena. Shutting his eyes briefly, he focused on the muscles in his back. He winced as the stretching and straining of his muscles began. Bones crunched and cracked as they grew out from the back of his spine. A pair of black, bat-like wings stretched out from behind him just as the vampire on the other side of the arena completed forming his.

Anton sprung from the rail and into the air, his wings carrying him over the troll and the graveyard. His powerful strokes shot him across the space, barreling him into the lesser who had just taken flight.

The pair flipped over the other in the air beneath the stalactites reaching down toward them, sending the pair cascading down to the sand. Dust rose into the air as the men grappled, pummeling their fists into the other. The lesser clawed into Anton's face, shredding his cheek with his nails.

A curdled shout ran from Anton's lips. The searing pain radiated through his gums and into his ears.

The lesser's blood-covered hands clutched around Anton's throat.

Anton shot his arms in between the lesser's and shoved his captor's arms from his throat. Anton stabbed his fingers into the lesser's eyes.

The orbs popped.

The lesser screamed as he clutched his bleeding face.

From across the arena, the troll's roar sounded, shaking the walls of the cavern. Anton glanced up at the stalactite ceiling. Some of the cones trembled, but none fell.

The lesser beneath him twitched and howled from the pain, blinded to the running troll eager for his next treat. Anton looked down at the pitiable creature below him and spread his wings. The troll was already halfway across the arena and picking up speed. Bending his knees, Anton leaped up and with a few powerful swipes was well above the troll's reach. While his cheek began to itch and twitch as it healed, Anton soared to the pathway he had earlier taken to head out on his mission.

Behind him, the lesser in the arena let out a blood-curdling cry. Anton smiled. The screams of the dying were now so sweet a song to him.

CHAPTER 8
A ROUND OF ALES

wen peered across the rolling hills toward the small mountain range rumored to be the home of the vampires. Lann was behind him, looking at the village that lie in between.

"It might be a good idea to actually interact with them, you know," Lann offered, uninvited.

Owen rolled his eyes. "How many times do I have to tell you, Airell said this is a *stealth* mission. I'm not to engage."

"You're not to engage with the *vampires*," Lann corrected. "But in order to gather more evidence, it's probably a good idea to talk to the people who likely *have* engaged with them."

Owen knew this to be true, but that didn't make it any easier. Even just thinking about talking to humans made his palms clammy. "I know. But what do you say? How do you engage with creatures who are so stupid they don't even bathe?"

Lann came up beside him and shook his head. "Mentioning their poor hygiene is probably not the best way to start. Why do you think so lowly of them?"

This was too much. Owen tightened his fists. "Why *don't* you? After what they did-"

"You cannot blame them all for what a few did," Lann interrupted, but his usual jovial features were gone, replaced by sorrow. "What happened to our mother...These people here wouldn't even know of it. Her death, the humans that killed her were in a completely different kingdom, far, *far* away from here."

Owen looked down. His heart sank. It was impossible to be comforted by the fact that his mother was among the ancestors watching over him.

I'd give anything to soar with her again.

"C'mon." Lann tapped Owen's arm. "Let's start by finding one of their pubs."

A drink did sound good. As he began to follow, Owen asked, "What's their ale like?"

Lann laughed and shrugged, "I think water is stronger, but, what can we do?"

The pair made their way into the stonewalled, thatch-roofed town. As they passed through the village, Owen saw that the market area, full of lightly stocked carts, was a lot like their own back home. However, even though there was no snow on the ground here, the vibe of the few people on the dirt streets felt equally as cold. Aside from the quick glances they gave Owen and Lann, they kept to themselves, hardly saying a word to even each other. Their nervousness bit at Owen's skin like needles. But what really stuck out to Owen, were the strange bird-like coverings many of them wore over their noses and mouths. He asked in a hushed tone to Lann, "Are they always so quiet like this? And what're those masks for?"

Lann shook his head. "No. They're scared. *Really* scared. Those masks, those are to help prevent the plague. They stuff 'em with herbs, which help to stave off the infection, which is smart. Let's just keep our heads down and try not to spook them, alright?"

Owen nodded. Passing through the town quietly sounded alright to him.

They wandered the mostly empty, dirt streets of the town until they followed their noses to a public house. When they stepped in, all conversations stopped. The few people inside turned to glare at them.

Owen gulped and froze in the door of the round-floored pub. The scent of dried rosemary filled the air. Owen noticed large bushels of the plant hanging around every three feet on the walls. The powerful aroma made his eyes water.

I wonder if these herbs are here to fight the plague as well?

Looking back down at the faces of the scattered occupants, some with masks dangling from their necks, some without, and others with them on their tables, Owen noticed how all of them tensed as if expecting something awful to happen at any second. Seeing the masks and the glares from the patrons in the dim light of the pub, somehow made them even more menacing looking.

Is this the look they give before they come at us with pitchforks?

A hand slapped his shoulder.

It was Lann with that ridiculous smile on his face. His brother motioned Owen inside toward one of the multitudes of empty tables. The pub could easily seat fifty people comfortably, but there were only eight inside, each with plenty of room at their own tables.

As they sat, the patrons continued to stare at them. Owen felt sweat forming around his dark brown hairline. With the back of his hand, he wiped his brow. He tried to lean back but the pressure of the concealed sword against his spine forced him to sit upright, increasing the tension in his shoulders and back.

Lann, however, leaned comfortably back in his chair, looking around the room. He held up his hand at a woman behind the bar.

The silence in the tavern was piercing. Owen couldn't keep still. He shifted back and forth, trying to keep his attention up, but his gaze low. Though the room was plenty large, he felt like the walls would swallow him up.

"What'll you have, lads?"

The woman's question made Owen jump. She'd come over without him noticing and now stood over their table with her hands on her round hips.

Owen's throat felt so dry.

"You travelers?" One of the men at a nearby table asked, leaning toward them. His leather mask with its long pointed nose was on the table beside his ale's horn. "I don' recall seein' you two around here before."

Lann looked at Owen, his head leaning toward the side.

Stars! I don't have a story.

"If you're travelers, why don't you lads have much with you?" Another man asked, making like he was going to stand.

What do we do?

Lann leaned over the table and said, "We had a bit of trouble on the road. We're passing through toward Dova on the other side of the mountain, but, I'll tell you, it's a good thing those *thieves* on the road were just happy taking our horses." He pulled out a small pouch that jingled as he dropped it on the table. "Otherwise, I don't know how we'd pay for a meal and an ale." His bright smile beamed and Owen felt the tension in the room drop a few degrees.

"You're lucky it was only thieves," the woman said. Her sternly pointed brows softened and she even smiled as she spoke. "How 'bout a pint and some soup for you boys?"

"Sounds lovely, thank you," Lann said. "And sorry 'bout

him." Lann leaned closer to her. His bright emerald eyes were practically glowing. "They ripped him off his horse and he fell right on his ass." He winked at her.

She chuckled and her cheeks flared red. "Don't worry, lad. Let me see if I can get you somethin' a bit stronger to numb your achin' ass and make you right again. Kiya." She snapped toward the bar. A young woman with red hair appeared from the backroom that Owen assumed was the galley. "A round for these lads."

Though he was sure the men continued to watch them, Owen leaned closer to his brother, his eyes wide. He couldn't think of a single thing to say.

Lann chuckled. He narrowed the distance between them. Just above a breath, he said, "People are generally good if you just take the time to get to know them."

"Tell us more 'bout the thieves," the man nearest them asked. "They only swiped your horses?"

Lann leaned back and sighed. "And all of our trappings we had stored on them. Figured they were trying to get the hell out of here." He shrugged. "Think we're all sort of running or hiding from the same things these days."

The tension in the room built once more.

What are you doing, Lann?

Lann looked around the room. "So few. Plague's been through here?"

One of the other men nodded and answered, "It swept through alright, but it's been some time since we've had an outbreak, thanks be to the gods." He gulped and shot a look down at his mask as if saying a prayer the herbs would continue to work.

Across the room, someone else sitting alone said from beneath his mustache, "The gods are dead." He chuckled. Many of the other patrons in the pub shifted, as if hoping a bolt of lightning wouldn't pass through the ceiling and strike them all for his blasphemy. As the man's chuckles calmed, he said, "It's the herbs what saved us. *Not* the gods."

Owen tried to remember what he had studied about the religion in the western half of Baradesh. The long, winding river that divided the country split the faiths as well. People in the east followed a monotheistic deity, embodied in the symbol of the sun, while here in the west, their religion was composed of seven gods. Owen bit his lips trying to recall them all, but he wasn't sure what good it would do if the balance of their faith was on the edge anyway.

Shaking her head, the older woman who was attending to them asked, "Are you boys...um, runnin' from plague or..."

Lann and Owen nodded. Owen sat up and tried to take the reins. This was his mission after all. "Our village has been swept through. Those who weren't taken by plague were taken by...well, *them*. We heard that the house of Dova, just over the mountains, is something of a safe haven."

All the men in the room laughed.

The young woman put the two horns of golden ale on their table. Owen watched the foam run over the lip of the horn placed before him.

"You're foolin' yourself if you think you can find safety from them," the first man said. A somber cloud took the faces of all inside. Some looked into their drinks, others toward the fire, none at each other. "Especially if you're tryin' to get over their mountain. It's just a matter of time before they kill us all."

"Jeremiah!" The man with the mustache who had spoken ill of the gods sent a look at the pub's owner.

Jeremiah shrunk down in his seat. "Dash it all, I'm *so* sorry, Della."

Oh no. Do they have someone she knows?

Della's large eyes began to well with tears, but Lann

jumped in and held up his horn to her. "Thank you for this, Della. Here's to all of our health and their damnation."

Some of the men chuckled, most held up their horns and drank.

Owen pulled the ale under his nose. The skunky smell of hops assailed his senses. He raised his brow and looked at Lann.

Lann laughed. "Just try it," he said behind the horn and took a gulp.

The men were watching him. The young woman who'd brought the ale was watching him. Della's enlarged eyes were on him.

Stars, how're they going to react if I don't like it?

Owen drew the cup to his lips and tasted the ale. It was sharp and made chills run down his spine. It was nothing like the creamy, dark ales they brewed and drank at home.

I thought Lann said their ales were weaker than water? This might punch the daylight out of a man if he had more than one.

Hoping not to offend the locals eyeing him from around the room, Owen threw it back and slammed his horn down.

Suppose I'll be seeing the underside of the table soon enough.

The men nodded and then returned to their own conversations, leaving the brothers be for the time being. Even Della nodded and returned to looking for something behind her bar.

"Lann, I think we have a problem," Owen started, looking into the bubbles in his brother's horn.

"What's that?" Lann took a sip, unfazed by the sharpness of the ale.

Owen said, "You know how in our trials we're supposed to help?" He flicked his head toward the nearest person to finish his sentence.

"Yeah?"

Owen leaned back in his chair. He could feel a tremendous

belch building in his stomach from the ale. After pounding his fist to his chest a few times, he said, "I don't think we're on the right mission. I think we ought to teach them how to make beer instead."

Lann laughed and shook his head.

The barkeeper returned with a glass bottle holding a caramel-colored liquid. "Here, lad, this'll help." She uncorked the bottle and poured a couple of ounces into Owen's emptied horn.

The scent made the hairs on the back of Owen's neck stand.

"One gulp of that'll make *everythin'* better," she assured, patting him on the arm.

"I'm sure," Owen drew the horn to his face. The cool vapors tickled his nose and the back of his throat.

This isn't beer. What is it?.

He threw it down. It burned like ice down his throat, followed by countless tiny pricks. His eyes watered as he coughed, doing everything in his power to keep the liquid down.

"Stars, I think I could blow fire with that," Owen said amid his coughs.

A few men around the room snickered as did Della.

"Della, there's only so many of us left, try not to kill these young blokes with your whiskey," the man nearest them said. He leaned back in his chair and resumed the game of bone dice he had on the table before him.

Della patted Owen on the back and said, "Nonsense, this'll make him stronger." She pulled out the third chair at their table and joined them. "What's your name, lad?"

His head was already beginning to feel light. Owen shifted his boots to be flat on the ground, steadying himself beneath the table. "I'm Owen, ma'am."

"And you?" She motioned to Lann.

"Quinlan, but, Lann'll do just fine." Lann sent a beaming smile at Della.

Owen wasn't sure if it was the tickling sensation tingling throughout him from the alcohol or if it was his brotherly disgust at Lann's charm.

"Listen, lads, I know you look pretty tough, but you're goin' to want to tuck in for the night. We don't have a proper inn here, but you can take my room. My daughter Kiya and I'll hunker down together for the night."

"That's awfully nice of you, ma'am," Lann started.

"Well, I'm not doing it for free." She motioned at his purse and he nodded. "But it'd also be good to have you boys around." She looked down and drew a circle on the table with her nail. The lightness in her eyes dimmed and her rounded shoulders dropped. "They...um, they took m' son. My oldest." She looked up, her eyes filling with tears.

Lann's eyes glistened as rested his hand on hers. "I'm so sorry."

It was clear to Owen that his brother genuinely felt awful for this woman. A part of Owen thought, *good, one less hunter,* but, this woman had already been so kind to them. She didn't even know them and was offering them a place to stay in her home. In her own room, no less.

Lann rubbed her hand then said, "They took our family too. What do you know about them? Anything?"

Della snuffled then started to answer, but the first man interrupted her with a hiss. "Della, we don't know them!"

She pointed at the door. "They came in here in broad daylight, didn't they?"

The man snorted then returned to his dice.

She shook her head then explained, "We're all starting to think the people in the east who think of the sun as their

56

greatest blessing might be on t' somethin'. That's one of the
only things we know about them; that they don't come in the
daylight, but I'm sure your people figured that out already."

Lann shrugged. "But that's all we have, really."

Della raised her shoulders. "I know other folks call 'em
vampires, but we're calling 'em raiders. They bite and they take
away our loved ones in the night. Being that we're so close to
their castle...when the nights are clear we can hear them...the
screams." She sucked in a sharp breath.

Owen's heart grew as heavy as a stone.

Della blinked rapidly and used one of her thick fingers to
wipe a tear from under her eye. "We pray our loved ones are
dead. Dead. We pray it was a quick death and that they're not
the ones we can hear screamin'. Awful, isn't it? Just awful."

Owen swallowed hard.

*Sounds like the prayer I had for my mother. I prayed it was
quick and that she didn't know any fear or pain.* He shut his eyes.
*But, is that what your kind gave her? Mercy as you killed her and
stole her from her family? How different could you really be, mortal,
from these vampires?*

"Now listen," Della continued, pulling Owen out from his
cloud of hate. "You boys might be tryin' to get to Dova, but if
you can, head all the way north to the coast, then follow the
mountains back down on the west side. Don't go through the
pass here. It runs right by their castle and you're only askin' for
death if you do."

CHAPTER 9
TRUST

"What is wrong with you?" Owen's voice hissed a moment after Della left them to stay in her room.

Lann raised a brow at his brother. "I'm not sure what you mean."

Owen bumped shoulders with his brother and explained, "How are you so chummy with them?"

Lann rolled his eyes. "Please. It's late. Let's just try to get some rest." Lann walked to the side of the bed and began to pull off his boots.

"It's not late, it's not even dark out yet." Owen crossed his arms over his chest, his shoulders aching with tension. Though it was early, his feet throbbed and his assignment weighed on his mind. He'd never realized mental stress could affect his body so. After rubbing his tight neck, Owen pulled his fur coat from his shoulders and laid it over his side of the bed as Lann had done on his side.

Lann undid the straps over his shoulders to pull off his sword. "A little tip," Lann started. "Don't sleep with this on."

Lann tucked the sword at the top of the hay mattress just above where his head would be.

Owen nodded and began to untie his leather straps while Lann was already tucking himself beneath the ox hide and their coats.

He's just trying to help. Why is that so hard for me to accept? But...these people. They looked like they wanted to murder us at first. Is that how they looked at my mother? She used to be chummy with them too. Stars, is Lann going to get us killed?

Owen sat on the side of the bed and contemplated his sheathed sword in the flickering light of the candelabra Della had given them. He gulped and his thoughts softened.

Della was so kind to us. What if Lann's right? What if they're not all monsters?

His shoulders drooped. He set the sword at the top of the mattress and started to say, "Lann, I..."

A knock on the door interrupted Owen. The brothers shot looks at one another. Owen stood and grabbed his sword. Beneath the door, Owen could see a shadow across the threshold.

"If you want answers," a young woman's shaking voice said through the door. "Meet me at the wooden bridge just west of town tomorrow after sunrise."

They waited until the shadow disappeared before speaking.

Owen gulped before he asked, "Do you think we can trust her?"

Lann shrugged. "I guess we'll find out. If she has more information than Della and the others shared, it could be very helpful for your mission."

Shaking his head, Owen sighed. "Why do you believe in them?" He put the sword back on the hay-stuffed mattress.

Lann set his hands beneath his head. "It's not just a black

and white matter of trusting or believing in all of them or not. I know it's hard, but you have to think of them as individuals, just like you do with our kind back home. Yes, mankind can be cruel, but so can dragons. Our duties, the reason we come down to help is so that the good ones can continue on and hopefully create more goodness in this world."

"Is that what you did?" Owen asked. "In your trial?"

Though the question was genuine, Lann shook his head and said, "Sorry, mate...I don't..." he shut his eyes as if trying to force the memory of it away. "I don't want to talk about it. Not tonight."

Owen bit his lip. "You're here to help me. You *fought* demons before and not just the common ones. You took on one of the seven *lords* of hell. What was he like? How did you fight him?"

"Owen," Lann snapped, sounding just like his father, which made Owen's eyes widen. "I don't want to talk about it. But what we learned in school about fighting them is all true; they fight without mercy. What they don't teach us about, is that they laugh at you while they kill you."

A chill ran down Owen's spine. "Stars. Did you see it? Someone be killed by one of 'em?"

Lann ran his fingers through his hair and said, "I said, I *don't* want to talk about it!"

Lann's raised voice made Owen lean away. He'd never seen his brother's cheeks flare red like this before. Lann pointed a finger in Owen's face. "If you ever come across one, you don't listen to them or give them a minute or they will kill you *and* they will take your soul. Do you understand?"

Owen nodded.

"Now, go to sleep." Lann settled back into his position, resting his head upon his arm.

Scooting his shoulders down on the mattress, Owen stared

up at the exposed wooden rafters and beams. Through the cracks above, he could see the light from the now empty pub. With an hour remaining before sundown, the patrons had departed for their homes, hoping to make it across their thresholds before dark. Owen shook his head. *How can anyone live in fear like this?*

He sent a sideways look at his brother. Lann kept twitching and moving about. *Why won't you tell me what the demons are really like? I understand they're scary, clearly, if the people are this afraid of the vampires who are probably products of demons. But how am I supposed to know what to expect if you don't tell me?*

Owen rolled onto his side, his back now facing Lann's. A heavy sigh passed from his lips.

You just want to be the hero, don't you? That's why you're not telling me. You just want to let me fail and then you'll sweep in and save me and that'll be yet another reason for everyone to worship you and think me a child. Or worse than a child. A hatchling.

A knot twisted in Owen's stomach.

I'll show you. I'll show all of you. I can do this and I'm going to prove it with the first vampire or demon we find.

CHAPTER 10
AT THE BRIDGE

A scream ripped Owen from his restless sleep. He bolted upright in bed and shot a look at Lann.

Lann remained on his back but his eyes were wide open.

"You heard it?" Owen asked, his heart beating against his ribs.

Lann nodded. "There've been a few. That one was the loudest."

Owen looked up through the floorboards of the pub, but only darkness stared back. "That can't have been all the way from the mountain."

Maintaining his pose, Lann answered, "I'd wager it was *very* nearby, if not in town."

"W-what should we do?" Owen asked. Though his hand was trembling, he reached for his sword.

Lann slapped his hand onto Owen's wrist, clutching his forearm. "Don't." Even in the shade of night, Owen could see Lann's crossed brows.

"What if it comes for us?" Owen asked, clenching his jaw. "We have to fight."

Shaking his head, Lann said, "No, Owen. It's not here. If you leave this room right now, you are *looking* for a fight. Your mission is to observe and only to intervene *if* necessary. We don't know where that scream was and we are supposed to keep a low profile. For the love of the stars, *please* don't do something stupid."

Owen ripped his wrist out of Lann's hand. "Why does everyone treat me like a child?"

"Because you are, Owen."

Owen felt every muscle in his body clench. As far as he was concerned, Lann could have just punched him and it would have hurt less than his words.

Lann ran his fingers through his hair then sat up. "The whole point of this, of the mission is yes, to prove balance and all that, but it's also to show that you *can* follow orders and eventually take your place as an equal member in our community. Do you even realize how many dragons have failed? That's why there are so many outcasts who live on their own. They didn't want to follow our kingdom's rules, so they went rogue. And father and I don't want that to happen to you. "

A large sigh escaped from Owen. He looked back up to the darkness between the planks and wondered, *Would it be such a bad thing? To be on my own if my own family doesn't believe in me?*

"Don't," Lann said again. "If you're thinking you'd be better off without your family, your blood, you're a fool. We cannot be in this world alone, Owen. Especially now. We are *far* stronger together." Lann settled back into the bed and rolled away from his brother. "Now, shut up, lay down, and go back to sleep. I'm sure we'll find out more about the scream in the morning."

Though he obeyed, Owen's stomach twisted. He reached

into his pocket and pulled out the necklace his mother gave him. Once more, tears filled his eyes as he rolled his thumb over the sun embossed in the silver.

Maybe I wouldn't have to do it alone. Mother, please help me to understand all of this.

⁓

THE NEXT MORNING, the idea of meeting someone by the bridge felt like a setup to Owen. It didn't help that the silent eeriness of the night following the screams, had kept him up all night.

"How can we trust whoever that was at the door?" he asked his brother, pacing the mouth of the stone bridge. The surrounding green, rolling hills, and the sound of the lazy river running by did nothing to calm him.

Lann shrugged. "Do we have a choice? And I don't really think it's much of a mystery as to who it was, do you?"

Owen ignored the question and continued to pace. Every now and then he'd glance up to peer at the castle in the cliff. The peaks of its black gates were just visible through the canopy of the maple and pine forest. A chill ran down Owen's spine.

We're still fairly far from it and yet I can see those gates as clear as day. How large are they? Did the demon's magic carve those gates?

A few minutes passed by before Owen asked, "How much longer should we wait?"

Lann raised his shoulders. "This is your adventure."

Owen tried not to curse, balling his fingers into fists instead. "If you're here as my mentor and I ask you a question, aren't you supposed to answer it?"

Lann held up his hands and said, "I'm sorry. Let's wait

another hour. The town is probably all stirred up after the screams last night."

This made sense to Owen. Though he wanted nothing to do with them, he did appreciate the chaos that likely followed once they realized one of their own was missing or dead. He looked to the sun peeking up over mountains that held their home in the east. They were but whispers on the horizon, but a dragon always knew the direction of its home.

I wonder what they would do if I didn't come home?

The hour dragged on. Owen had just about finished counting all the stones lining the river's edge beside the bridge when a familiar form approached, her red hair blazing in the morning sun. Owen dashed back across the bridge to join Lann who'd been meditating alongside the path.

"It's Kiya, right?" Owen asked his brother under his breath.

Lann peeked his eye open and peered at the young woman approaching. "Was it really that much of a mystery to you?"

Owen snorted. "I just want to make sure I remember her name."

Kiya waved quickly at them, her shoulders drawn high and her gaze darting back and forth. She joined the brothers at the side of the bridge's entrance and began to speak. "Sorry I'm late," she started, her voice quivering. "Another one of ours was taken last night. Least they killed her though." Kiya drew her arms across her chest, tucking them close.

"I'm so sorry," Lann said.

Owen nodded. He bit his lower lip then asked, "Was it someone you knew?"

Kiya shrugged. "We're a small town, you know? We all know each other, care for each other. The worst part of it is waitin' until the morning t' find out what happened. We hear the screams, but we can't do nothin' f'r fear of being killed ourselves, then we feel like dyin' until we found out what happened, you know? But, look, I don't have much time 'fore I'm missed. About a month ago, one of our regulars came in and told me that he'd almost died of the plague. He's the first in a while to have had it and he said he was dyin' and then one of...*them* came in. To his home. A woman."

Owen motioned her to go on.

Kiya pushed away a strand of her hair from her face as she continued, "Said that they saw how sick he was and he thought she was gonna kill him or that she was gonna take him back to their lair to..." She trembled as she finished her sentence, "To make him *into* one of them. She took him from his home and carried him to a homestead about a day's walk that way." She pointed north-west from where they stood. Owen figured it was near to the base of the mountain. "And then she healed him."

Owen felt like he'd been slapped. "She what?"

Lann raised a brow.

"Healed," she reiterated. "'Parently that's something they can do. So, he said she healed him. He spent the next couple of days with a few other people being feed and cared for by this woman. She even had him escorted home, makin' sure he was alright. Said she told him not to tell anyone about them healin' him or even that he was sick, but he wanted me to know in case m' mum or brother got sick."

"About *them*?" Owen asked. "Is there more than one performing healing?"

We can heal ourselves, but we can't heal others. What sort of magic is this?

Kiya thought on this a moment before answering, "I really don't know. Mum interrupted us 'fore he could finish." She dropped her head. "I wonder if...if m' brother could be there with her." She looked toward the cliffs and motioned toward it with her brow. "I can't stand the thought of him bein' there."

The brothers looked to one another, but before they could ask any questions, Kiya continued, "Please, go to the cabin and talk to the woman. She's supposed to be very kind and might be able to give you some answers. If you do, could you ask her if she knows about m' brother?"

Owen's stomach tightened. *That means we have to come back and deal with these people again. Can't we just leave and be done with them?*

"What's your brother's name?" Lann asked without hesitation.

Kiya's hazel eyes lit up. "Byram son of Ofguard and Della."

Lann nodded and took a step closer to the girl. "We can't make any promises, but we will try to find out what we can. Be careful, Kiya, and stay safe."

Kiya nodded to the brothers then set back off toward her village.

Owen drew a circle in the dirt with the round toe of his boot.

"What's wrong?" Lann asked. "We have a lead."

It wasn't the notion that they'd have to come back if they found any information regarding her brother that bothered Owen. It was the fact that yet another family had been devastated and there was nothing he could have done to stop it.

Humans or not, what's the point of us being down here if we can't do anything real to stop it? Why does the council have to get involved? Can't we just act?

Owen ignored his brother's question and the ones rising in his heart. "Let's go." Owen continued across the bridge and field, following Kiya's direction in silence, his brother right behind him.

CHAPTER 11

A REMINDER

The sound of the woman's screams intoxicated Anton. They were almost as sweet as the blood.

Anton sunk his teeth deeper into the man who lay in the bed beside hers. His meal kicked and squirmed and punched at his head, but Anton's teeth were deep in his neck. Though the man's moving about was annoying, it did not take away from the fine taste of his blood.

"Stop! Please stop him!" the woman in the bed behind him screamed.

Anton smiled, his lips moving across the man's neck as he pulled and supped.

The squirming of the man began to slow. Anton could feel the man's heart pounding against his chest, sending gobs of blood flooding into Anton's mouth. It was far more than he could eat and his belly was already full, but Anton kept his extended fangs planted in the man's neck until finally, the beats slowed. Then stopped. He withdrew his fangs.

Anton stood, gazing around the room. The woman who

had been screaming at him now wept great shuttering sobs that racked her body. Aside from her, eight other people stared at him with wide eyes in this log cabin's infirmary. They all sat straight up in their beds, all looking more like ghosts than warm-bodied mortals.

This infirmary was yet another one of his ideas. The people feared plague, but they knew nothing about how to protect themselves from it, save for praying to gods long dead. Once the vampires realized the potential healing power of their blood, Anton suggested the soft-hearted Riva take the ill under her care in this cabin, heal them, before sending the healthy ones up to the castle for their lord to decide if they should be lessers, greaters, or meals like the man he'd just drained.

Feeling his meal dripping down his chin, Anton smiled and pointed to the blond woman standing with her hands tucked to her sides. "You're doing an excellent job at healing them, Riva." Anton's voice hummed.

Anton looked at the lifeless body of the man he'd just drained, blood running from the puncture wounds and pooling beneath the body. Anton smirked while he said, "Taking a bite of this man was just a little demonstration. A reminder that these people here are nothing more than our sheep." He swept his arms around, pointing at all of the trembling people inside. Then, he motioned toward the lifeless body on the bed in the middle of the cabin. "A reminder to you, Riva, that you are taking care of our lambs before sending them on their way to slaughter."

With the heel of his palm, Anton wiped away the blood still dripping from his chin, smearing it up his cheek. One of the sheep's skin went gray.

The man's gagging made Anton chuckle. "What? Do you not like my mask?" He approached the man quivering so much,

Anton reckoned his teeth might fall out. He bent over the man and spread the sticky, warm blood up over the man's nose. "Isn't it better than those silly bird masks you all *clearly* failed to wear." He stood straight and extended his arms. "Which is how you find yourselves in our charitable arms." He chuckled. "You'd be *dead* without us."

Anton crossed the hall to the doorway where the woman he'd known his whole life stood. Instead of staring at him like the rest of them, her eyes were straight down on the worn wooden planks of the cabin.

He shook his head. With a soft touch, Anton pulled her chin up, making her eyes meet his. "And once they're done here. They come to me. *Yes?*"

Riva's blue eyes looked into his Anton's a moment, before whispering, "Of course."

"Every. Single. One?" he growled.

Riva nodded.

"Good girl." Anton leaned forward, pressing his lips to her ear. "And if I hear that they aren't coming to me..." His tongue ran down her neck, his grasp on her jaw tightening. "You'll get to join our other friends who have failed in the arena and the troll will see to your delicious end."

Anton released his grasp and stood beside her. With a bright smile showing, he extended his fangs. She shuddered.

Anton turned to the people still quivering in their beds. "Your futures are bright! If our lord finds favor in you, you'll have work, food, a roof over your head, and the *undying* protection of my family." He clapped his hands together once, making everyone in the room jump. He sighed. "Now my little lambs, I must go." He started to walk out of the room.

Riva's wide eyes searched those of all the people in her care, pleading with them not to say a word.

They all heard the front door open and close loudly, but Riva kept her gaze firm.

The heals of Anton's boots stormed back into the room as he said, "How silly of me, I shouldn't travel that far without a snack."

CHAPTER 12

BROTHERS

"Get down!" Lann grabbed his brother's shoulder and dropped him to the ground.

The screams erupting from the cabin ahead echoed in the forest. The brothers stared at the long log cabin nestled away by a river in the woods. It had taken them all day to find it and now that they had, Owen wished they hadn't.

The brothers peered through the long arms of ferns they hid behind across a dirt road from the cabin. By the moon's light, they saw that no horses stood by, and as far as they could see, whatever horrors were happening were happening inside.

"We have to help them," Lann started. He began to stand, but Owen grasped onto his shoulder, pulling him back down.

"You said yourself last night that we're not supposed to intervene and -"

Owen's sentence was cut short when the door to the cabin burst open. A man emerged, dragging a limp body behind him. A woman followed, stopping in the doorway as the man hauled the body to the grass before the cabin. She extended her arms across the frame as if hoping to shield whoever else was inside from this leaving terror.

The man turned toward her and tossed the seemingly lifeless person upon his shoulder as a herder would a lamb.

Owen gulped.

Think it's safe to say we found a vampire. Stars, they're strong.

The darkness of the night concealed the details of this man from them, but they watched him head off down the road on foot, taking his limp prisoner with him.

The woman remained on the patio, waiting until he was a ways down the road before returning inside and shutting the door.

This is my chance.

"We have to follow him," Owen stood, beginning to pursue the man.

"Owen, wait," Lann started after him.

Lann's brief words made Owen's muscles tighten. "Wait? You want *me* to wait? You were about ready to blast in there blind! He's alone. We can take him."

Lann shoved his brother into the rough bark of a pine, the flat of Owen's sword pressing hard into his back. "Look, Owen, I was stupid to try to rush in there. We don't know he's alone and so what if we eliminate *one* vampire if that is what he is? As far as we know, there are *many* more. We need to learn more about them before we can fight. I'm willing to bet that the people in there will have more information."

Owen stabbed his brother in the chest with his finger as he hissed. "No, you look. This is *my* trial and I'll lead it as I please." Owen peered around the bark of the sticky pine. Owen pushed his brother away and strode off in the direction of the man with his captive.

"Owen, we can't." Lann followed. "We have to talk to the

people in there first. We don't know what the vampires are capable of."

Owen ignored him. Though the man was now out of sight, Owen was determined to follow the road until they found him.

Just keep going. This is my time. We are dragons. We can trap that vampire and get answers from him. One way or another, he'll talk.

"Owen, stop!" Lann's hand latched onto Owen's arm. "Don't rush into this just because you want avenge Mother."

Red flashed before Owen's eyes. His other hand swung around in a fist, right for his brother's face.

Lann ducked, still holding on to his brother's arm, pulling him down toward the ground. Owen's fist lost its momentum but collided with Lann's shoulder.

The brothers tumbled to the earth. Owen rolled on top of his brother and instantly began to hit him. Rage filled him and fueled his punches.

Lann held up his arms, shielding his face and deflecting Owen's blasts.

As far as Owen was concerned, this person before him wasn't his brother. It couldn't be. How could his flesh and blood want to spend time with people after what people did to their mother? That woman in the pub last night, she was alright, but the others? Maybe the vampires were sent here to punish them for their sins. Maybe they deserved the terrors they were enduring.

Owen's fists continued to bash into Lann's forearms, his knuckles bruising as they hit Lann's flesh and bones. He threw a punch and missed, his muscles beginning to burn.

Lann suddenly shot his body upward, rolling Owen off him and pinning his back to the ground. Lann grasped onto Owen's wrists, holding them on either side of his head.

Exhausted and out of breath, Owen's narrowed eyes

screamed his hatred. The look cut through his brother harder than any of his blows.

I could do it. I could turn to my natural form right now and there would be nothing left of you and your love for those monsters.

Lann leaned back, his grasp weakening. "Owen?"

A white light slashed through the trees, blasting Lann from atop of Owen, spiraling him off into the surrounding bramble.

CHAPTER 13
THE WITCH

"Lann!" Owen sat up. Sweat poured down the sides of his face as he stared out into the empty forest. The moon seemed to be against him, casting more shadows than light across the forest floor.

Owen pushed himself up from the ground, staying low. He searched the shrubs and bushes that surrounded him, but still no Lann or sight of their attacker.

"Stand up," a woman's voice commanded from behind.

Owen shot his eyes toward the cabin.

Not twenty feet away, stood a young woman with her arm extended. Even in the low light, Owen could see the stick she pointed at him.

And that must be a wand.

"Stand. Up," she repeated, keeping her wand aimed at his chest.

Which means you're a witch whose magic might be as powerful as ours.

Owen slowly stood, holding his hands at the level of his

ears to show he was unarmed. "What have you done with my brother?"

"You don't get to ask questions." Her focus was so tight on him. She ignored the slight breeze which blew loose strands from her long black braid into her face. "Who are you? Why were you hidin'?"

"We didn't feel much like getting carried away by that man," Owen motioned toward the direction where the vampire had gone. "We're just people. We're not vampires."

"Why were you fightin'?"

Owen looked down. *Because your kind beheaded my mother and used her scales as armor and my brother wants to be chatty and friends with you all regardless.*

"Because we're brothers!" Lann's voice shouted from somewhere nearby.

Hearing his brother's voice, Owen forgot about the wand pointed at him. He moved toward the voice, but an invisible fist punched him in the side, dropping him to his knees. A tingling, biting surge hit his body, whipping his hands behind his back restraining his wrists with an invisible rope.

The witch approached. As she neared Owen, she said, "I'm sorry for all this, but we have to be careful these days." She pointed her wand and flicked it toward her.

Lann's body popped up from the ground and levitated toward Owen, his arms similarly bonded by an invisible rope.

The lady before them looked to not have reached twenty years of age yet. She was young but in control. Her dark eyes focused on them both.

Even in the moonlight and with her weapon pointed at them, Owen felt his throat dry in the same way it did when the lovely warrior Airell was around. Clearing his throat and shoving the thought aside, Owen said, "W-we heard the screams. We wanted to help."

"Ha!" She looked them both over. "How? Doesn't look like either of you have a sword or any sort of weapon that might take on what we're facin'."

"We *have* to try," Lann insisted.

Her brow raised. "We *have* been tryin'. In our way, at least."

"By helping people?" Owen asked.

She considered them, pursing her full lips together tightly. "Look, I don't want to let anyone near our home unless we know we can trust you. Prove to me you're not vampires."

Lann and Owen shot their gazes to one another.

"And how would you like us to do that?" Owen asked. His heart was pounding. The only way he could think to do that would be to assume his dragon form, which he would never do before a mortal. The threat of being banished aside, it was too dangerous. Especially in front of one as powerful as a witch.

She bounced on her heels a moment, her long wool coat swaying against her calves. "I could leave you outside until dawn, see how you fare in the sun, or..." Her lips turned into a smile. "Here's an idea." Reaching into her coat, she pulled out a knife with a carved wooden handle. "One of you slice your finger on this." She tossed it in front of the brothers. "But don't try anythin' stupid. One wrong move and you're both dead." The wand in her hand remained steadily pointed at them.

Owen looked at the knife. "What'll this prove?"

After shrugging, she said, "The sight of blood seems to be intoxicatin' to vampires. They can' resist it. If one of you is bleedin' then the other will dive for it. And, for the other who is bleedin', well, if you start healin' immediately, well, we'll know you're one of 'em."

Though his throat felt like it was lined with dirt, Owen gulped. He thought he might as well just turn into a dragon now.

She's going to know.

"I'll do it," Lann said.

What're you doing? We heal, you cloud-headed fool!

But the challenge had already been accepted. The young woman nodded and then flicked her wand toward Lann. His arms released from their invisible bonds. Without wasting a moment, he picked the knife up from the ground. "It's just a little cut, Owen," Lann assured. Owen knew he was trying to tell him more than he was saying, but that didn't help to ease the tension in Owen's high-held shoulders.

Owen watched his brother take the blade, which was as long as one of their hands to his palm.

Oh no, Lann. I know what you're going to do. You're going to cut deep enough so it takes longer to heal. Stars, that's going to hurt.

As if anticipating the same thing as Owen, the woman stepped forward and said, "Wait, you don't have to -"

Lann sliced the length of his palm. Lann winced. Blood poured out. His knuckles holding the blade went white.

"Stars," Lann whispered, sucking his lips in tight. He looked up to their captor and then back to his brother, blood still running from his hand. "Have we passed your test? I think I'd like to wrap this now." He tossed the knife to her feet then pulled his hand tightly back to his chest.

She rushed to Lann, kneeling before him, setting her wand in her lap. "Let me jus' look really quickly, then I *promise* this'll be over." Lann extended his hand to her, biting his lower lip as he did. Owen tried not to look, but how could he not? The slit in his brother's hand was clean, bright red blood pooling around it in his palm. The woman swallowed, pale in the moonlight, waiting to see that he wasn't already healing.

"Fine, fine, I believe you." She reached back under her coat and pulled out a white handkerchief. As she wrapped Lann's hand with it, she said, "Neither of you looked the slightest bit hungry with that anyway. Truth be told," she chuckled. "You looked as sick as I felt." When she finished wrapping Lann's hand, she picked up her wand and flicked it at Owen, releasing him from his bonds. "I'm Helen," she introduced. "And I'm sorry I had to put you through this. We jus' don't know who to trust these days."

After standing, Owen looked down to Lann who was clinging to his wrist, staring at the wrap around his hand that had blood seeping through.

He's probably already healing, but it's sure going to hurt for a while. He could have had me do it, but he didn't, even after I beat the daylight out of him. How much of a cloud-headed git am I?

Owen tapped his brother's shoulder and he offered his hand to help Lann stand. Lann nodded then placed his uninjured hand in his brother's, joining him on his feet.

Taking in a deep breath of the cool night's air, Owen tried to get his heart rate to level out before he said to Helen, "I'm Owen. This is my older brother Lann. We've been trying to find out more about them, the vampires. You seem to be familiar with them, to say the least."

The witch smirked and the tension in her shoulders dropped a little. "I'd say so. Want to meet one?"

The brothers exchanged looks again.

"Is she the one who's been helping people?" Owen asked.

Lowering her wand, the witch answered quietly, "Tryin'. She's tryin', but with surprise visits like this from Anton...well, why don't you two just come in? I'm sure we'll have much to talk about."

They began to follow the witch out from the tree line and toward the cabin. She checked their surroundings before she continued at a whisper, "I was out collecting herbs for our stores when I heard the screams." She motioned to the pack she carried over her shoulders. "Screams only mean one thing - Anton was here and he's damn lucky I wasn't here for whatever hell he brought tonight. Riva's the vampire inside, 'least, I hope she's still inside. She's been set up here by their leader to gather people sufferin' from the plague, to save them, and in exchange, they go to the castle and serve the lord of the vampires."

"Who is their leader?" Owen asked.

Helen shook her head. "I don't really know, but that man who just left is his second in command and he's a murderous little prick."

"How are you involved in this?" The sharpness in Owen's tone made the witch turn on her heel to face him.

With a mere hand's distance between their two noses, she said, "This was *my* family's cabin. Anton murdered my parents in front of me. Said I would be Riva's pet and do her biddin' unless I wanted to see my little sister dead. He had me and a few others clear out what little trappin's we had from my family's grand room to make room for the beds he wanted for the sick.

"I *hated* Riva at first, but now that I see what she's doin', I'm doin' everythin' in my power to help her. Someday *I* will be the one to take on Anton and stop all of this."

Owen scoffed. "You think *you're* going to stop the vampires?"

"I stopped you two, didn't I?" She continued to the cabin and didn't say another word to them, even after she opened the door. She motioned at them to enter.

The second the brothers stepped over the threshold, the metallic scent of blood assailed their senses.

CHAPTER 14
REVERENCE

A fair-faced woman emerged from the open door across the room they entered. Her expression, framed by her golden halo of hair, was stern at first, but softened when she saw the witch. "Who are these men, Helen?"

Closing the door behind them, Helen said, "A pair of brothers I found fighting each other like thistle-headed fools in the woods."

Owen tried not to smile. It was the first time he'd heard one of them use a phrase similar to the one they used back in his homelands.

Helen continued, "They wanted t' meet you, Riva."

Owen looked around. The front room they entered was humble, with not much more than a large iron stove, a table covered with drying herbs, various sized jars, and a bed barely big enough for one person shoved in the far corner. He tried to see through the only other door Riva emerged from, but a white sheet was strung across the opening. The small, fresh smears of blood on one side of the sheets did not comfort him any.

Riva approached, her blue gaze narrowing on them. Owen could almost hear his brother's heart beating faster. There was a different energy about her than he'd experienced from any of the people they'd yet met.

Her brow raised as Riva asked, "Are you wizards?"

Can...can she sense that we're not really what we seem? Like how I can feel there's something different about her?

Lann answered, "No. Are you a vampire?"

The question deflected her. She rotated her shoulders and said, "Yes, but before I answer any of your questions, can I ask you to help us?"

Owen opened his mouth to argue, but Lann cut him off. "What do you need?"

Riva motioned with her hand toward the door behind her. "My superior just came through and absolutely..." she held her breath and her eyes lined with tears. "He made a demonstration to remind me that *he's* in charge."

Helen went around them and peered behind the sheet. She immediately retreated, covering her agape mouth with her hand. "*Damn* him," she growled.

The brothers followed Helen's lead and pulled the sheet back. On one of the tightly laid out beds lining the walls was an occupant who would clearly never walk again. Though the face had been covered with sheets, blood soaked through the fabric. Owen's stomach turned. He tried to breathe, to keep his last meal down, but the metallic smell was overwhelming. Trying to stay focused, he looked at the remaining people in the room. Pale faced, silent, and wide eyed, they looked like their very souls had been broken.

"Please," Riva's hand landed on Owen's shoulder. He jumped, but she was unmoved. "Please help me bury them. They didn't deserve this." A tear ran down her cheek as she looked back into the room. "None of them do."

AFTER THE INITIAL BURIAL CEREMONY, Helen returned inside to prepare dinner for the occupants inside. While they finished laying the man to rest in the small cemetery behind the cabin, Riva explained to the brothers how she became a vampire and about the demon that controlled them all. "I knew I was making a deal with a demon, but I'd just watched my entire family be destroyed, my whole town." Tears ran down her cheeks and her shoulders shook with sobs. Taking a deep breath, she drew the shape of a sun in the dirt over the man they'd buried.

Owen thought of the necklace his mother had given him. *The sun. She's drawing a sun. Even though she's damned, she's drawing a sacred symbol of the people in the east. I thought they worshiped multiple gods and not just the sun over here. Interesting.*

Riva continued to draw as she said, "I've done what I can to try to fight it from within, healing these people with my blood and then sending them home as quickly as possible, but Anton, that *monster*...he's been dropping by more and more lately. He took inventory tonight of the people inside. It's the first time he's done that. Now that he knows who I have..." she hiccuped a sob and sat on the earth between the fresh mound and an older grave with small white flowers and tufts of grass growing on it.

I wonder if that's one of Helen's parents.

Lann knelt beside her and rested his hand on her shoulder, while Owen rested his arms on top of the standing shovel they used for graves.

The burial ceremony had fascinated Owen. First, they'd wrapped a cloth around the man's head, while Helen said, "*We close the mouth so your soul may stay with your body during its transition to the next life. May the god of the underworld accept your body as a worthy gift, and may they assign your soul to a higher birth than this."* Then the four of them carried the body outside for burial.

Even though Helen could've used her wand to move the body or to dig the hole, she'd said that laying someone to rest was a sacred act requiring reverence and one's hands.

Owen watched their procedure and traditions unfold with wide eyes. It had been so different than anything he had seen before. When dragons passed on, their brothers and sisters would set their fallen brethren before the sacred stone. In their dragon forms, their community would gather around the dead and rest their hands upon the body in silence. Then, in the evening, they would throw a tremendous feast in honor of the deceased. The feast would last for hours before the final ceremony. The body would be carried to the northern side of their mountain, a small valley that, on clear days, could see all the way to the sea in the north. There, the dragons would raise a tremendous pyre. A beloved of the deceased would set the flames and the body would slowly turn to ash, flakes filling the sky. The living dragons would stay up all night, watching their loved one join the stars.

Trying to force out the bitterness inside him that they hadn't been able to give this ceremony to his mother, Owen cleared his throat then asked, "What do they do with them? The people they take from here?"

Riva sighed and looked up to the heavens above. "Some become lessers. They're turned into vampires and have to earn their way up into various positions, by doing the bidding of the shadow lord without question. But until they ascend, they are slaves at the mercy of greaters like Anton who've earned our lord's favor. Most are just meals or playthings." She drew in a shaky breath. "The *least* fortunate end up in the arena."

"What's that?" Owen pressed.

"It's literally an arena inside the mountain's castle. The lord likes to entertain himself by watching mortals or lessers fight various animals or mountain trolls. The trolls are his favorite, for they know no mercy or fear and rip the mortals and lessers apart." She shuddered. "It's horrible."

"How do we stop them?" Lann asked. "How do we stop them from filling up this *whole* valley with corpses?"

While Owen had been entrapped witnessing the traditions of these people, he was glad Lann was asking these questions; the more they learned now, the sooner they could finish this and go home.

Maybe we really won't have to go much farther than this cabin. We haven't been gone long at all and I'm already missing our mountains.

Riva raised her shoulders. "I don't know how to stop them. If I did, I would have died trying already."

Owen pulled in a deep breath then said, "What're your strengths? Any weaknesses? There has to be something that can help."

Lann continued to sit beside Riva, his eyes glistening as if he was captivated by her every word.

Riva thought a moment before saying, "Um...well, aside from the fact that we can fly and we need blood to survive -"

"Hold on," Owen held up his hand, interrupting Riva. "You can fly?"

Riva nodded. "It takes great concentration, but..." she shut her eyes. "If we focus on the muscles in our backs and, I'm honestly not really sure how it works, but...we can sprout wings. Enormous, black, bat-like wings."

Owen's jaw dropped. *They're shifters too?*

"It's how Anton and the shadow lord's followers are able to take so many people away and disappear in the night." Riva continued, "They take off with their victims in flight." She motioned toward the windows and crossed her arms over her chest. "The screams you've probably heard at night? People think they come from the castle, but they're from people being carried toward the mountain with the wings of death above them." She wiped a tear from her cheek. "Um, we, er, we get cold, we get hungry and tired. We bleed, but, we heal and can heal others if we're careful. That's what I do here. If we give *too* much blood, well...whether they drink it or it's transferred, too much of our blood will turn them into us.

"I think the *one* true thing we are learning to fear is sunlight. We're *very* sensitive to sunlight." She rubbed her hands together slowly as she continued, "It's like how infants shouldn't be in the sun because their skin is so fragile. Our skin burns and it burns *fast*. I imagine a vampire could die from exposure if left in the sun for too long."

"What about fire?" Owen asked. Lann shot him a look that cautioned him to be careful. "What if we tried to burn out the castle?"

Riva shook her head. "There are several people in there, *good* people...but..."

"But what?" Owen pressed.

Her eyes searched the ground as she pieced together her thoughts. "That might make sense. That might be why the demon really keeps mortals there. To keep people or us vampires who he knows resent him from trying an offensive like that."

A part of Owen wanted to transform right now, fly up to the castle and destroy the damned place, good people inside or not. But his father's words cautioning him against such an approach rang in his heart. His shoulders dropped.

Mother would never forgive me for doing something so awful.

"Do you mean to face them?" Riva asked Lann. "The pair of you? Is that why you're asking these questions?"

Owen looked to Lann. His soft smile and raised eyebrow encouraged Owen to answer. Owen nodded. "We come from a...village that's fought demons for years. The more we learn now, the better prepared we'll be to stop this shadow lord and his followers."

Riva leaned away from Lann. She looked back at the cabin where Helen was tending to the people inside. "If you do, I don't think you would have to do it alone."

CHAPTER 15
QUESTIONS AND ANSWERS

The sun's light shone through the branches of the forest's trees. Owen shut his eyes as he stepped out of the cabin into the crisp morning air, letting the sun warm his cheeks.

I don't think I've ever appreciated this as much as I do now. To think, Riva might never be able to experience this again.

Owen opened his eyes and continued on toward the shed with the chickens. Exhaustion dragged on his arms and legs, but before going to sleep, Riva had asked him to help Helen with the chores. The survivors from the vampire's castle had spent the night awake, with all of them keeping a sharp watch on the forest while the healing people rested. Now that dawn had reached her hand across the valley, Riva and Lann would rest first.

Owen liked the idea of being outside the cabin, though he'd never had any prior experience with chickens. He'd consumed many, of course, but never paid much attention to how they were kept back home.

The soles of his boots crunched along the length of the

cabin to the side opposite of the small cemetery. The clucking of chickens came from the small fenced in area with a thatch shed.

Is Helen inside there?

Owen opened the pen's wooden gate and headed toward the triangular building's door.

Do I just go in?

Gulping, Owen reached for the door's latch. "Helen? Are you in there?"

"Yes," her voice, muffled by the walls of the shed, called. "Come in and help me with these eggs."

Owen's shoulders relaxed and he pulled open the door.

A flash of talons and white feathers flew at his face.

Owen ducked as the flapping bird cawed and cackled as her down fell against his body. Among the calls of the chickens, Owen heard Helen laughing.

"I'm so sorry!" she said through her chuckles.

Owen felt his cheeks flare red. The chicken who'd flown at him proceeded to strut past his ankles and out to the pen.

"What'd she do that for?" Owen asked as he brushed a number of feathers from his chest.

Helen pulled the woven basket closer to her stomach as she said, "I suppose she was excited to see you. You have a little something in your hair." She pointed at his head.

He swiped his hair and watched a few tiny feathers float down in the air. Around him, the other chickens resting on their perches seemed to not have a care in the world. "Why couldn't she be like them?"

Helen chuckled and said, "Well, they're all different. She was just feeling a bit feisty this morning. Now, I've already just about finished this side. Could you get to work on those girls there?" She pointed at the row of chickens in their hay nests, sitting in a line level at his knees.

Owen counted nine in this row, though a handful of them jumped out of their nests the second he took a step forward, following their feisty friend to the pen. He nodded then looked back to Helen to see how it was done.

He watched Helen scoot her hand underneath the grey-mosaic feathered belly of a hen, whispering and cooing to the girl as she did. In a smooth motion, she pulled out a green egg and placed it in her basket.

That doesn't look hard at all.

Owen kneeled before a brown hen. Her shiny, black eyes gazed at him from beneath her red comb.

You're not too different from a dragon, are you, mate?

Extending his hand toward her belly, Owen whispered, "Hiya, girl, I'm just going to reach in here and -"

Her feathers raised.

Owen's hand stopped.

What's she doing?

Seeing that she didn't do anything else, he gulped then continued his reach.

The tip of her yellow beak stabbed into Owen's knuckles.

"Stars!" Owen ripped his hand back to his chest, while Helen's laughter echoed out once more. He looked up to her while the chicken before him released a hum of a growl.

This chicken's even more like a dragon than I thought.

"I'm sorry," Helen apologized again. "You don't have much experience with them, do you?"

Owen smiled as he rubbed the throbbing spot where the chicken pinched him. "Whatever gave you that idea?"

Helen shook her head and then kneeled beside him. "This one's a bit pecky, but she won't really hurt you." Without flinching, Helen reached under the chicken, taking three hits from the bird's beak, and pulled out two brown eggs. "There, see?" Helen gently placed the eggs atop the others in her basket. She patted him on the shoulder then returned to her side of the small coup.

Now knowing the worst of what to expect, reaching beneath the chickens to collect their eggs became an easy chore for Owen. As he pulled an egg from an empty nest, a question rose to his mind. "Um, Helen, might I ask you something?"

From behind him, she said, "Well, you could ask the chickens, but I don't think they'd answer."

Owen chuckled then asked, "If vampires need blood to survive..."

"What does Riva eat?" Helen nodded. "That's a fair question. She can eat what we eat, but *their* blood." She pointed at the chickens. "Sustains her. She says chicken blood's not the same though, like, while it fills her it doesn't quite satisfy the itch she always has for our blood."

"Isn't that sort of scary?" He reached for another nest.

Helen raised her shoulders. "It was at first, especially when Anton first brought her here. He said that I was to serve as her occasional meal while she healed the others." Owen's brows reached for his hairline, but Helen continued, "One of the reasons why I started to like Riva was, she was healin' people, but she wasn't eatin'. She wasn't givin' her body what it needed to survive. She was dyin'. She might've too if I hadn't cut myself for her."

Owen almost dropped the eggs in his hands. "You did what?"

"She was dyin'. As far as I was concerned, she was the only light the sick had. I saw how she was fightin' Anton, sneakin' the healed out as she could. You fight for people like that. So, I didn't give her a choice. I cut my forearm and presented it to her."

Owen slipped the eggs into the basket that was set

between them before he asked, "Weren't you afraid though that she might lose control? The way you thought we might if we were vampires last night?"

Helen shook her head. "No. I had faith that she would do the right thing. And she did."

The weight of her faith in someone others would consider a monster sat on Owen's thoughts like a mountain.

Helen sent a bright smile at him then said, "C'mon now, there's more work to be done."

"WHEN RIVA SAYS she heals with her blood and they have to consume it, how much does it take? And could she heal them all at once? Why do they have to stay here so long?" Owen asked Helen as she used the magic from her wand to chop potatoes on the table. The idea of consuming blood as medicine made his stomach turn, regardless of how well the soup Helen was preparing smelled.

Helen sent a sharp gaze at him, the bottomless depth to her black eyes making him light-headed. "I'll answer your questions if you contribute." She pointed at the other knife on the table and at the row of rosemary beside it.

Owen picked up the knife and began to chop the herb. *She's probably gettin' tired of me. I've been asking her questions all day.*

They had spent the day together, making meals for the sick, checking in on them, cleaning the cabin, and while it had been a lot of work, Owen found, to his surprise, that he had enjoyed it. Of course, it helped that Helen was at his side the entire time.

Helen motioned with her wand and the sliced cubes of potatoes flew from the table and into the iron pot's steaming soup.

Owen's feeling of nausea dissipated as the salty waft of the chicken broth she'd made overnight filled his nose and made his stomach growl. As she continued to use her magic to add vegetables to the stew over the fire, Owen smiled and asked, "So is this what witches brew looks like?"

She shot another sharp look at him then rolled her eyes. "Ha, ha."

Her magic fascinated him. It was so different than that of his kind. He'd learned about the magical capabilities of witches and wizards when he was in school, but it was a totally different thing to actually see it.

"T' your earlier question about the blood, we don't know the *why* behind it, and they're just given a small, a *very* small amount, which is why they still have to stay under our care for a while. If they're given too much of her blood...well, they can turn. That's how the lessers *first* started."

"How did the vampires figure out they can heal people?" Owen asked. The chopped rosemary before him lifted with her magic from the table and landed in the soup. "Seems like the vampires are more determined to kill mortals, no?"

"Try not to make those pieces so big and crush it with the side of the knife, that'll release the oils, which heal as well." Owen looked at the knife and then pressed the side of the metal upon the sticks as she answered, "I don't know. I just take people and try to make their time here comfortable while I can."

"How do they get chosen? I mean, who decides who goes to the castle and who gets to go home?"

Helen's shoulders dropped. She looked to the door where the people were recovering both physically and emotionally from all of their trials. "Well, if Anton had his way, we'd send them *all* to the castle. Riva decided to fight by keepin' some of them alive, but the choice was impossible...so, to keep it fair, it's a draw."

"A draw?" Owen stopped chopping. "Like gambling?"

She nodded. "Whoever draws the black stone goes." She used her magic to bring an onion onto the table before her.

"So the vampires at the castle...they don't know who's coming beforehand?"

Helen's spell began to chop the onion into quarters. Its stinging scent made both of their noses run. "No." She snuffled, but Owen wasn't so sure it was just because of the onion. "We leave it to fate so no one has to choose. It's *awful*, trust me, you have no idea what it's like taking people up to that place knowing that they'll never come out, but I have *no* choice." Helen's round eyes locked with his. Though their discussion was as heavy as it had been all day, there remained to be something about her that stole him away from his discomfort around mortals, tucking him into a safety that he had not known since before his mother died.

Clearing his throat and wiping his palms, which suddenly felt so clammy, on his pants, Owen asked, "They have your sister there, don't they?"

Helen set her hands on the table and leaned forward. "They show her to me each time I take people there. They say it's so I know they're keepin' their word keepin' her alive, but I think it's Anton's way of reminding me *they* are in control."

Owen nodded. He leaned back and looked into the room of healing people. Lann was in there with Riva, talking with them and doing his best to calm them. Though the people were terrified, the gratitude they had expressed to him and his brother for helping to bury a man who was a stranger to them stayed with Owen. Here was a room full of vulnerable people, waiting to be healed and possibly carted off to their doom, but none of them argued or tried to take out their anger on Riva or Helen.

They kept their kindness toward the ladies and thanked them for providing all the comforts they could.

Owen adjusted the soft fur collar around his neck then looked to Helen. *You cloud-headed fool. They deserve so much more, so much better than this.*

"So how do we take back control?" Owen's voice asked before he had a chance to really think about what he was saying. Helen's raised brow made him bite his lip, realizing how idiotic he sounded, but still he persisted. "Riva said you might be willing to join us...our village, that is. If we...*when* we fight them."

Helen shook her head and pulled on the end of her braid. "I don't know. My family's no stranger to fighting demons. With our powers it's something we've been shepherded toward for generations. There was a time when we were so strong...but these vampires...*they're* stronger."

Seeing her lip quivering as she struggled to find her next words gave Owen the sudden overwhelming urge to hold her in his arms. Instead, he cleared his throat and set his hand atop hers.

Helen shot her gaze up to his and for a moment, Owen felt like he was flying again.

She lightly tapped his knuckles with her other hand then drew away. "I suppose, strong as the shadow lord is, all demons have a weakness. His, I suspect, is light. *Strong* light. That's why his progeny, the vampires are so sensitive to it, and why he keeps in a hole so deep underground, but I don't know how we'll actually *get* to him."

Owen picked up the chopped onion and dropped it in the pot. The steam that rose out from the bubbling waters filled his senses. He stared into the rising vapors as an idea began to surface.

"When do you have to take your next offering to them, Helen?"

Helen narrowed her brow and then answered, "I have to be there by tomorrow night. Why?"

"I think I know a way for us to get inside."

CHAPTER 16

TAKING CONTROL

"It's mad," Riva said after listening to Owen's plan.

"Hear me out." Owen knew he sounded like a thistle *and* cloud-headed fool, but his instinct felt like this was right.

Their group of four gathered around the table in the kitchen whispering to one another so the people behind the sheet would not hear the plan. Laid out before them on the table were tiny sticks from their dinner's herbs, which Riva had arranged as the basic schematics of the mountain's castle.

Owen licked his lips, pointing his index finger beside the schematics, as he explained, "Helen takes Lann and me up there as an extra special offering, an apology or something, to show the shadow lord your fealty. Tell him you found us, you think there's something special about us, and then once we're in, we'll be able to take care of the demon, while you and Helen go in and get the good people out."

"You certainly think highly of yourselves," Helen said, rolling her eyes. Her arms were crossed tightly across her chest. "We don't know how many would be willin' to leave with us, which means we don't know how many will stand up for the shadow lord, and, need I remind you, he's not just any old demon. He's a *lord* of hell."

"With mountain trolls," Riva added.

Owen could see Lann holding his breath as if waiting for him to have to clean up Owen's mess. He glanced at his brother's hand, still wrapped to conceal his palm, which had likely healed at this point.

You're not the only one with good ideas, Lann. I'm not going to tell them we're dragons and that we have a fleet of dragons who'd come to join us.

Owen shrugged then said, "Look. We've fought demons too. Well, Lann has."

Riva's brows were so high Owen wondered if they'd be able to come down. She pinched the bridge of her nose and said, "Owen, it's very kind of you to try, really, but...look, let's keep working on this. I think you're on the right track. How long did you say it'd take your village to make it to us to help?"

Owen bit his lower lip. He hadn't. This was something he wished he'd asked Lann to help him cover. *I know this was supposed to be an observational mission only, but how can walking away help anyone?*

Looking to his brother, Owen raised a brow, hoping Lann might fill in what he was missing.

Lann crossed his arms over his chest then slowly answered, "We'll have to send word to them. And they'll have to discuss it prior to joining us, but, our people *are* warriors, dedicated to driving demons back to hell."

Riva responded at the same speed as Lann's answer, "This, again, is very sweet of you, but, Owen, really, but let's say, best-case scenario, we get in and are able to start this attack... what if your village *can't* join us in time? How far away are they?"

"They will join us," Owen affirmed, hoping to avoid answering the second question. He looked to Lann again, but his brother would not meet his eyes.

Why won't you support me on this?

"Regardless," Helen started. "If their people are with us or not, we have to ensure that Anton does *not* escape."

Riva nodded. The tension in her shoulders eased slightly as she said, "I've known Anton his entire life. He's *always* been wicked. I found out not too long ago that on the night when it all started, he was supposed to bring medicine to try to save his parents. They were wealthy, they were connected, they might've had a chance...but he chose to save his own life. I suppose we all did, but anyway, Anton was destined to deal with hell one way or another. While he's currently the shadow lord's left arm, I think he'd stab him in the back at the first opportunity he could if it meant he might take over. We may accidentally *help* his cause if we're not careful."

"What demon did you fight?" Helen asked Lann, cutting Riva's argument short.

Shutting his eyes, Lann hesitated as if his words had been stolen from him for the first time. "I really don't..."

C'mon mate, you're a legend among our kind for what you did.

"Please," Helen insisted. "We need to know what you've dealt with before we agree to anythin'."

"I um..." Lann started, keeping his gaze toward the table before them. "Alright. I was out east trading when I came across a town where they'd been dealing with Gallu demons. Are you familiar with them?" Lann ran his fingers through his hair.

Helen nodded. "They're the dead. The bodies of those poor fools who sold their souls in life and in death must serve their masters."

Owen looked closer at his brother's eyes and realized they were beginning to line with tears.

Lann again ran his fingers through his hair as he continued. "When I arrived, the town was in chaos. The Gallu were ripping people apart. Their lord, one of the lords of hell, probably not unlike our shadow lord here, was strutting through the center of the town, his bony arms up in the air. I'll never forget what he looked like." Lann shut his eyes. "Grey skin. Giant black sores. Sunken eyes. And all of his teeth were fangs."

Owen had never heard Lann tell the tale of what happened. He'd only ever heard the other dragons toasting his success or gossiping about how brave he had been.

"He was laughing as he was telling people to swear their alliance to his king, to the king of the damned." Lann cracked a soft smile as he continued, "They didn't. The people *refused*. I think seeing what happened to the Gallu, seeing their skeletal bodies with flesh dangling off, reassured them that surrendering to death was far less a consequence than giving up their souls." His smile faded. "But...there was a baby crying, screaming her head off. The lord of 'em was going toward the hut where the child was. Stars know what he was going to do if he got to her. I came out from where I'd been hiding and I challenged him." Lann's words flowed faster and faster like he needed them heard to cleanse his soul. "We fought...and I... with a swipe of my...sword I took his head and sent him back to the fires of hell."

Riva's and Helen's jaws dropped. Owen's stomach rose to his throat.

Did you really use your sword? Or the razor-fins of your tail to take on a monster like that?

Lann pressed his fist to his lips as he started, "Ending the rest of the Gallu was easy enough after that."

The women stared at him.

Lann sighed then said, "We grew up in the mountains of the east. Dealing with demons are an unfortunate curse of our birthright. We learn early on how to fight and how to send them back to their king." He patted Owen's shoulder and said, "His plan? I think it'll work *if* our village can join us. We'll contact them right away. We have...mates nearby who could help us deliver the message quickly. Once they're here, get us inside, then get everyone, including yourselves, the hell out. Leave the rest to us."

Riva snorted. "I'm sorry, this is all very brave, truly, but let's think on this a bit more. Demons you know. Vampires..." she shook her head. "We don't even yet know the extent of what we're capable of."

Owen leaned his fists onto the table then pushed away. Muttering he needed a bit of air, he walked out into the night.

CHAPTER 17
RIVERSIDE REVELATIONS

Owen's feet hadn't crossed much of a length before he heard the door open behind him. He had hoped to take a quick walk around the forest that surrounded the cabin, maybe even to go sit beside the river's edge, but Lann's voice called out his name.

Owen slowed his pace, but he did not stop. He was already beside the small cemetery and halfway to the water.

I just want to sit by the river and look at the stars for a while. Is that too much to ask?

"Hey, mate." Lann placed his hand on Owen's shoulder and gently turned him around. Owen didn't want to look at his brother but dragged his eyes up anyway. "We need to talk."

Owen's brows popped up toward the sky.

Shaking his head, Lann said quietly, "Owen, you were, *we* were specifically told on numerous occasions that we were to be observational *only*. The core of your mission was to scout out information and then report *back* with the understanding that if you *were* confronted with a demon, you'd take care of it. This, what we're talking about doing, is *well* beyond the scope of your mission. You're talking about sieging the castle *tomorrow*." Lann threw his hands up in the air. "I don't know that our 'village' will make it in time."

"I can't believe this," Owen planted his fists on his hips. "So, now that I'm finally starting to think these people aren't a bunch of cloud-headed, murderous monsters that actually do deserve our help you're saying, we shouldn't?"

Lann shut his eyes. "No, Owen. That's not what I said at all. I just don't think your timeline is going to work out. We need to notify our village *now*. We will need their help."

Do we? You fought a lord alone and a village full of demons alone. How much harder could vampires be split between the four of us?

Owen shook his head and started to walk away from his brother.

"Owen," Lann started, any hint of his normal joviality was gone. "I know what you're going through."

"Do you?" Owen scoffed. "The *hero* of our time?"

Lann shot his gaze down to the knee-high grass they stood within. "Do you want to know why I never talk about what happened on my first mission?"

Owen flicked his nose up to encourage Lann to go on.

Kicking his toe into the dirt, Lann said, "You remember the baby I mentioned?"

A sudden weight filled Owen's stomach. Lann had mentioned a baby, but only that she was crying. He never said what happened to her after he fought the demon.

"I thought I could do it," Lann's eyes met Owen's. "Be a hero on my first trial. So I waited to act. Instead of notifying our village that I was in over my head with a town full of demons, I watched. I wanted to learn how they fought so that when I did go in, I'd be ready. What I should have done was call for backup and not thought that I could do it all alone.

"I taunted the lord and lured him to the forest, running with all of my might. Once I was sure I was out of sight, I changed. I'd barely finished when he attacked me. It was brutal. I can't even tell you how long we fought, or how painful it was when his claws ripped across me."

"How did you finish him?"

Lann glanced back over his shoulder. He leaned close and whispered, "Got lucky, really. Caught him looking the other way for just a breath. I cut his head off with the fins on m' tail." Lann leaned back then ran his fingers through his hair. "Stars, I was so stupidly happy. I thought I'd done it. That I'd won.

"When I got back...I'd killed the demon lord alright, but his Gallu were still in the town and..." Lann shoved his fist against his lips. He was shaking. "She didn't make it. While I was off playing hero, a monster stole that little baby from this world. I should have called for help instead of trying to to be a hero. If I had maybe...she might've made it. More people might've survived if only I had done things differently.

"That's why I've gone on so many missions. I want to try to save as many as I can, but I know that I will *never* forget that girl's screams and I'll never make up for my mistake of letting my arrogance get ahead of my duty. That's why I almost ran in here blind last night. I don't know, it just...it sent me right back to that village."

Owen took a few steps away from his brother and leaned against the wide trunk of a red cedar.

"I always wondered why..." Owen shook his head. "Why you never talked about it."

"You're smart, Owen, and very strong," Lann started. "But please, let's notify our kin before we go running in there. We need help. You know the elders will still have to consult on what to do. It might take time for them to respond. I know this means we'll lose someone tomorrow. *Trust* me, I understand how hard that is, but we just don't have a choice. If we do this right, we'll have a far better chance at ridding the world of this evil."

Following the back end of a sigh, Owen nodded. "Do you mind doing it?" He didn't think he could bring himself to change into dragon form so close to a house full of people. In order to notify their kin, using their own fire, they would send up a series of smoke beacons that could be seen for miles and miles around. The humans were used to the smoke from hearths, but they were not trained in the patterns signals every dragon knew from a young age. The dragons who were nearby, the same who left their trappings at the beginning of their mission would see it, even in the dark of night, and would race to the mountain to notify the elders that help was needed.

"Alright," Lann said. "Go back in whenever you're ready, then tell the ladies that I went off to meet our mate. This shouldn't take me long." Lann closed the distance between himself and his brother. He rested his hand on Owen's shoulder. "It's not easy, but it's the right choice."

"Yeah, yeah, go on," Owen's words dismissed his brother, but, he smiled. "Thanks, Lann."

Lann nodded, then headed toward the road. Once Lann was out of sight, Owen set off on a walk to clear his mind. The cool night air kissed his cheeks as the soles of his boots crunched on the pine needle and leaf litter carpet beneath them.

Owen found a log covered in a variety of mosses so green, he could see their vibrant colors in the moon's light. He sat atop the log, setting his fingers atop the soft mosses, and stared up at the moon.

Is this the right thing to do, Mother? Owen reached inside his pocket and pulled out the necklace. *Is waiting to fight the right choice? Please, show me a sign.*

From behind him, Owen heard footsteps approach. He shot a look over his shoulder and saw Helen.

"May I join you?" Her voice rolled over him like the softest of furs.

Owen looked over his shoulder, watching her figure move in the moonlight. He gulped.

"You know...join you." Helen pointed at him. "On the log?"

Owen popped up and nodded. *Stars, she must think me a fool.* He shoved the necklace back into his pocket. While he had wanted a moment to be alone with the stars, his heart lightened with the idea of Helen as his company. *She's as fierce as Airell and just as kind.*

As she settled onto the moss pad beside him, she said, "I can't believe how much has changed so fast." Her dark eyes turned up to the star-speckled sky.

"What do you mean?"

Helen chuckled. "Well, let's see. Within the course of *one* day, two strangers show up at our door and not only think they're capable of fighting demons, but are actually trained in how to do it along with a whole village of other people. After the hell we've all been through, isn't that alone sort of a miracle?"

Now Owen laughed. "Some miracle; two brothers who woulda beaten each other senseless if you hadn't intervened and don't really have any solution for getting you all...*us* all out of the mess tomorrow. But didn't you say your family has been fighting demons for some time?"

Helen nodded. "Yes, but we haven't really been trained. We just fought. There's a difference." She pointed toward the mountain. "Before the vampires and the plague came, there was talk of a school openin' up on the other side of the mountain at the house of the Dova family. They're a powerful line of witches and wizards whose school might make a difference.

They say it'll be one to regulate how witches and wizards are taught so our children could harness our true potentials. It'd given us the tools we'd need to really fight the demons. Sounded pretty nice, but then..."

"The world ended?"

She laughed. On the back end of her laughter, she said, "Well, I don't think we're quite there yet, but it's certainly been turned upside down."

Owen smiled, but his heart felt heavy. While he was starting to see the goodness in people, he wanted to ask her something to feel like he really was making the right choice. "You still think there's goodness here? Good...people?"

Helen raised her brow. "Well, yes. Don't you? We all found each other, didn't we?"

Two dragons, a vampire, and a witch. What an odd sort of group we are.

"I s'pose so." For a moment, he looked to the moon, then returned his gaze to Helen's. Once more, his spirit felt as light as it did when he was soaring through the skies. "I'm really sorry they have your sister, Helen. I don't know how we'll do it exactly, but I'm not leaving there until we get her out. You are one of the good ones and I'm willing to bet your sister is too."

Helen's eyes welled with tears, but she did not let them fall. "Thank you." She asked, "If it's not too nosy of me, what were you looking at before I came over?"

Owen bit his lower lip. *Should I show you?* Owen decided there was no harm in sharing and pulled the necklace from his pocket. "My mother gave me this." Holding it out in his palm, he continued, "She said it was to remind me that we're all connected. All the same."

Helen ran her fingertip over the sun as Owen had done on countless occasions. "I know this symbol well. My parents worshiped the sun as well." She snuffled then asked, keeping her gaze down. "What happened to her? Your mother, I mean."

Owen held his breath. He'd never imagined having to ever tell a human what happened. Biting his lower lip, Owen considered what to say. "Um...she um..."

Helen placed her hand on his shoulder. "I'm sorry, I shouldna asked. That was stupid of me."

Shaking his head, Owen continued, "No, it's alright. It's just...it wasn't that long ago. She was out and as far as we know, she was, um, robbed and murdered on the road. Beyond that, we don't know who did it or why. M' mother really loved to help people and yet -"

"So that's why," Helen interrupted.

Crossing his brow, Owen flicked his nose at her to explain.

She raised her shoulders and said, "Why you and your brother are so kind. Sounds like goodness runs in your blood."

Owen had never thought of himself as being kind. He was only here because of the mission from his elders, and yet, a desire was growing so brightly within him to help that the only explanation he could reckon was from his mother's love. Owen snuffled and looked up to the stars. "I suppose you're right." He smiled to the heavens.

Thank you for the sign, Mother.

Owen brought his gaze to the necklace in his palm. "Take it."

Helen's eyes met his. "I'm sorry?"

Owen placed the necklace in her hand and closed her fingers around it. "You said yourself, the demons and vampires took everything from you. This, what this represents, they can't take that from you."

Tears welled in her eyes. Helen leaned forward and kissed his cheek.

An electric tingle erupted from Owen's face and ran

throughout his body. He barely noticed when she stood and moved away, saying, "Thank you, Owen, truly. I'm going to try to get some rest. Dawn'll come soon enough."

Owen nodded, focusing on the warmth her lips left on his cheek.

It was just a thank you kiss. Don't get your tail tied in a knot over a human kissing your cheek.

He looked back up at the moon and smiled. *I'm starting to see it now, Mother. Why you cared so much for them. They really are just like us.*

From behind him, Owen heard soft footsteps approach once more.

What'll I do if it wasn't just a thank you kiss and she's coming back for more?

Gulping, Owen put one of his hands behind him, so he could turn around on the log to see her. Instead, what he saw curled his hands into fists.

CHAPTER 18

FALLING

A shadow person gazed at him from behind a tree. The deep silhouette's eyeless stare sent a chill so deep down Owen's spine he thought he might never feel warm again.

Owen planted his feet in the earth. He reached up over his shoulder and drew his short sword from behind his back.

The shadow whipped behind the pines, dashing so fast among the surrounding trees, Owen's eyes could barely keep up.

Owen bolted off after the shadow, sword still clutched in his hand. His heart pounded as he chased the shadow deeper into the forest.

Stars! Are there more of them?

The shadow doubled then tripled time and time again. They'd shoot up beside him then dart away so quickly, he couldn't even raise his arm to strike.

Stopping his run beside the river, Owen clenched his fingers around the pommel and growled, "Cowards! Why don't you face me?"

The shadows stopped. Ten stood, with arms at their sides, ten feet away, as still as the trees that framed them.

Owen gulped. He could see the reflection of the moon on the lake shimmering through the silhouettes before him.

A thump fell right behind him. Owen spun around, but a balled hand bashed into his brow with a force he had never known. The sword flung out of his hand as he cascaded toward the earth. Owen's face bashed into the hardened mud. Stars filled his vision as a pounding ache sprung to life on his brow where he had been hit.

Owen tried to reach for his sword, blindly patting his fingers on the earth, trying to feel for the pommel.

Fingers grasped the hair on the back of his head, ripping Owen's face from the mud. Owen reached back, trying to find the attacker's hands. His feet kicked beneath him.

"Let me go!"

His captor pulled him flat against his own body and clutched his other hand so tight onto Owen's neck, he fought to breathe.

"Scream for help," a male's velvet voice whispered in his ear, his lips caressing his skin. "And I'll kill them all."

Anton.

Anton threw Owen back to the earth with a force that knocked the wind from his lungs. Before Owen could draw in any breath, Anton pressed a knee onto his back, sending waves of pain shuddering through his body. Owen flailed his arms and tried to flip around, but Anton leaned his knee harder between his shoulders.

You don't have a choice. You're not strong enough as a mortal. Turn into a dragon, kill him or he will kill you. No one will know and you'll be able to go home. It'll be alright, just do it! Owen shut his eyes and began to concentrate on the spell.

Anton pulled Owen's head up from the ground with his

hair and slapped something hard and cold onto his face. Owen tried to rip the iron mask away, but Anton had already locked the device around Owen's neck.

"What is this?" Owen demanded, his voice muffled by the mask that fit from the bridge of his nose down to the tops of his shoulders. Owen's heart sank. It was now far too risky to transform into a dragon, for the iron could strangle him.

"Insurance," Anton answered. Releasing his grasp of Owen's hair, Anton stood. "Get up."

Owen's shaking arms pushed him from the ground. Over the top of the metallic-smelling mask, he could see he was surrounded by a tight circle of shadow figures. Anton stood before him wearing a smirk that intensified the coldness of his cobalt blue eyes.

"Insurance?" Owen asked, hoping that maybe if he could buy time, Lann might stumble across them and end this.

Anton's smirk turned into a sneer. "You see, we vampires have a tendency to bite." He snapped his teeth in Owen's face and chuckled when he saw him flinch. "These masks help to prevent our lessers in training from getting out of hand. They also have the benefit of adding a layer of shame, which, I thought I might use on Miss Riva tonight, but this...I think I like this better. And now, you're coming on a little walk with us."

Anton snapped his fingers and the shadow people fell upon Owen, binding his arms so tight behind him, his shoulders felt dislocated.

"And if I don't?" Owen growled, struggling to fight the shadows.

Anton's brow crinkled. "Your friends die. And you watch." Raising his shoulders, he asked, "Is that not enough motivation for you?"

Owen looked back toward the direction of the cabin. *Why*

didn't I follow Helen back inside? He turned his gaze back toward Anton and nodded.

"You made the right choice." Anton began to walk off in the direction of the mountain. The shadows shoved Owen so that he would follow. "Oh, young sir, I'm so excited to take you to our charming home. And I'm quite certain you're just *dying* to see it too."

CHAPTER 19
IN THE DARK

The chattering of his teeth roused him from a dreamless sleep. A moist cold bit into his skin, reaching through his blood and muscles, chilling his very bones.

Owen blinked hard. Sharp, stinging pains radiated throughout his body. The last thing he remembered was being brought before the gates of the castle at the belt of the mountain. A vicious wind had gnawed at his eyes over the iron mask as the doors opened. He had tried to peer inside, but Anton spun about and struck him in the head once more. Everything had gone black.

Stripped of his furs and boots, Owen wore nothing but his hide trousers, soaked from the moisture in his cave prison. The iron mask was gone. No chains or lashings of any kind restrained him. Gingerly pushing himself up from the wet stone floor, Owen gazed around the tight space surrounding him. An iron-barred door entrapped the plain walls, which had been roughly carved from the black stone. Points of rock jetti-soned out at him from the walls and ceiling like knives threatening to cut him. Owen had never before felt more trapped or helpless. Sitting flat on his rear, he didn't even need to fully extend his arm to poke at the tiny stalactites above his head.

And here I thought my chamber back in my home was small. Stars, what a fool I was. I could try to make my transition and become my true form, but I'd likely break more bones than bars in the process.

Though his muscles ached from the abuse he'd sustained on his passage to this place, Owen pushed himself forward toward the iron bars. Soft tufts of his breath's mist flowed from his lips. Attached to the wall of the small hall across from his cell was a single, burning bowl of oil. He could see that his enclosure was raised a few feet above the pathway. Owen estimated that the base of his space would come up to the height of his hips. There looked to be a similar iron-barred gate across the thin hall, but, as far as he could tell in the dim light, it was not occupied. Pressing his aching face to the metal, he tried to gaze down the hallway, but between the darkness and the angle, all he could see was another wall of rocks.

I wonder how deep within the mountain they have me?

His fingers gripped around the cold metal. He tugged and pushed, hoping they might budge, but the heavy-linked chain trapping him within would not shift.

Owen bit his lower lip, but recoiled, realizing it too was sore.

What did they do to me? And what sort of monsters are they, beating me while I was out cold? I didn't even have a chance to fight back.

He shut his eyes and listened. The silence weighed upon him like chains, but, after a moment, he could faintly hear the sounds of moaning and...his eyes opened.

"Screams."

As if they'd been waiting for him to become aware, the

screams scratched their way down the rock, echoing louder and louder with each one.

Owen gulped. He pushed himself as far away from the door as he could, concealing himself in shadow. He sat, tucking his knees to his chest, shivering in the darkness. Nothing came to alleviate the stillness of the cold, save for the occasional scream.

Owen tried counting the sharp points in the ceiling, but his shivering kept him from focusing. Time began to slip away. In the silence, Owen's regrets weighed as heavily upon him as the iron mask had.

I should have listened to Lann. I should have gone with him to send the signal to our kind. Anton might still have come, but at least I wouldn't have been alone.

The sound of boots coming down the hall roused Owen from his reverie.

Owen's face popped up. He tightened every muscle in his body and prepared himself to fight.

You are a dragon. No matter what comes, do not let it overcome you.

A bright, flickering light approached. Both of Owen's eyes strained as the fiery torch passed before his iron bars and stopped.

"Hello there," a young man's voice called through the bars. Owen didn't have to see him to know that this was Anton.

"You never left, did you?" Owen's hoarse voice asked through his cracked lips. "That's why you were there."

Even in these hellish conditions, Owen could see how Anton remained spoiled in life, wearing a silk cravat pinned to his jacket with an emerald.

"You are correct," Anton answered. "Why leave? I was sent to keep an eye on Miss Riva and how could I do that if I wasn't there?" Anton ran his eyes up Owen's body. "Yes, I think you'll do well."

"In what?" Owen was having a hard time dismissing the blood boiling in his veins. *I could do it, I could harness my dragon, change, and take him out with me. I'd be a hero, but I wouldn't be able to celebrate it.*

Anton tilted his head to the side, then peered down the hall before answering in a whisper, "To help me, of course."

Owen's brows shot up. "You beat and kidnapped me, you sold your soul to a demon, and you're a murderer. Sorry, mate. Not interested."

Anton laughed and rocked on his heels before whispering, "So certain? Is big brother the thinker and you're the muscle?"

Owen leaned back.

Smiling, Anton said, "Oh yes, I heard all of that and about your little village too. I'm sure your people will have a *ball* coming in here trying to save you."

Stars, he heard that, but...he said people. We never said we were dragons. Owen's heart started to race. *We may have a chance.*

Anton snorted. "Ah yes, you do care about them. Your heart is screaming that so loudly. If you choose not to help me, I will relish drinking their blood for weeks. I assure you though, I won't let any go to waste...well, mostly." He smiled and extended his pointed fangs. After sliding the tip of his tongue over them, he said, "I'll ensure you'll have a front row seat, that you last for weeks and weeks and weeks, until everyone you love is gone. Or, you can join me, I'll let them in, I'll let them *save* you, and you all may go out back into the world on your merry ways."

Riva's warning about Anton looking to make a power move against the demon rose to Owen's thoughts. He narrowed his eyes. "What do you want me to do?"

Anton nodded. "That's better. If you are *such* a warrior as you believe you are, this should be easy for you." Anton checked the hall again. Holding the torch close to his face, Anton whispered, "Win in the arena. Kill them *all*. The shadow lord will be so impressed with you, I am certain he'll think he's found his ticket back into the graces of hell. All you have to do is keep him focused on you. I'll take care of the rest." Raising his shoulders, Anton said, "That's it."

Owen crinkled his brow. *What sort of bargaining chip does he think I am for his lord?*

Anton chuckled. "Why so concerned?"

"It seems...too easy," Owen answered.

With his brows up, Anton said, "Let's see if you still think that with a mountain troll swinging a bat at you." He smiled wide then continued, "I will say, there's something..." Waving his hands in front of him, Anton looked like he was trying to put his finger on the word that he could not find. "I don't know...*different* about you and your pretty silver eyes. I noticed that of you and your brother. I beat the senses out of you and yet, here you are, without so much as a bruise." He ran his eyes over Owen's body once more. "Or a scar. It's really quite remarkable. You may actually survive in the arena if you can heal like we do.

"So, if I've timed this correctly based on your little heart-to-heart with your brother, your brother will come in with your little villagers, they'll take on and hopefully send the shadow lord back to hell, and all the meanwhile, I'll take what I want and you all will leave. Do you understand?" A shadow crossed over Anton's face that sent a chill down Owen's spine. "You will not come for me. You will *never* come for me. Understand?"

Nodding, Owen asked, "What do you want out of all this?"

Anton leaned back from the bars and once more gave a glance toward the exit. After leaning back toward Owen, he said, "My parents were monsters. People *are* monsters. We killed our gods and then blamed them for our plights when the plague fell. I don't believe in gods. I don't believe in people. I believe in power.

"Did you know that demons can ascend within hell? That they can *earn* their way up the ranks to sit at the table with the king of the damned?" He pointed up as if motioning to the demon in the mountain. "Our lord *fell*. He failed to do the bidding of his master and now he's trying to earn his way back. I...*we're* a part of that. He's hoping he can spill enough blood and give his king enough souls to earn his way back to one of the seven thrones." Anton shook his head and leaned closer to the bars once more. "What do *I* want? I want to beat him to it." He smiled then said, "Have fun in the arena."

CHAPTER 20
LESSERS

A growing light accompanied the increasingly loud rattling chains. Owen moved himself to the far end of the cell as he waited to see what was coming.

Two men emerged from the hall wearing long, black robes. One threw a pair of boots in front of the cell. From under their hoods, they peered between the iron bars.

"Come on now," the taller one started, motioning toward the door. The men both looked to be around Owen's age. "It's time for you to come out. You'll be fightin' in the arena today." The heaviness in the man's voice told Owen that he took no pleasure in his present duty.

The shorter man pulled a ring of keys from his thick cloth belt and began to unlock the chain on the gate.

They don't have armor. They're barely wearing anything beneath those robes and neither have a weapon. I could take them both easily and try to slip out.

Slowly, Owen made his way toward the iron bars. As he began to plot his escape, he met eyes with the taller man. Owen could feel in his heart that the guard felt sorry for what was happening to Owen and to all of the prisoners he'd collected before.

Sweat formed on Owen's brow. He wasn't worried about being injured in the arena, for he knew he could heal, but he had to survive long enough for the healing to start.

And then what? If they keep me here long enough, they're going to figure out I'm not a mortal man. Do I dare just change now? But if I do, I'll never be able to go home again. I can't do that. I want to go home.

The guard began to unwind the chains from around the thick bars.

Maybe I could just knock these two out and then try to escape. No, Owen. Don't be a fool. Stick to the plan and don't hurt anyone who's a prisoner as much as you.

Once the chain was freed, the guard opened the gate and stepped aside, waiting for Owen to emerge.

His legs felt like lead as he stepped out from the space and into the hall. He hadn't been able to stand up properly in the short niche he occupied. He stomped his bare feet against the stone floor trying to regain feeling.

The taller man motioned toward Owen's wrists and said, "Put on your boots then put your hands up, and *please*, don't try anythin'. We don't want to hurt you, but...we don't want to be hurt either. Understood?"

Owen nodded. He leaned down and pulled his boots onto his feet. It was such a relief to have his warm shoes covering his cold toes and ankles once more. Once finished, he held his wrists out forward. The men bound him in iron shackles and, standing on either side of him, proceeded down the hall.

At least I'm not in that iron mask again.

As they tread past the other cells, a memory rose to Owen's mind. Turning to the guard who had been speaking, he asked, "Do you know if a Byram is in here? Byram of um..." Owen's silver eyes searched the uneven stone floor as he tried to recall what Kiya had said by the bridge. "Oh! Byram son of Ofguard and Della?"

The tall guard shook his head. "I dunno. I can tell you he's not either of us, but..."

The other guard continued, "We recently changed are just addressed as lessers. We aren't encouraged to speak to each other much and we only know the names of all the greaters and I can assure you, 'e isn't one of them."

Owen didn't know if that was comforting or not, but decided to hold on to the hope that Kiya's brother might be down here alive.

I wonder where they'd keep Helen's sister. Stars, I hope she wasn't ever in one of those small cells.

The hall turned up and to a curved flight of stairs. Torches lined the walls, toning down the cold ever so slightly as they climbed the stairs.

"How big is this place?" Owen asked, his voice echoing in the tight pathway.

The shorter guard answered, "The shadow lord says we can fit five thousand people in here, but I dunno about that."

As their stairway entered another hall, Owen tried to imagine how the demon managed to carve this place out from the mountain, but the sounds of the screams from earlier were increasing with every step forward, dragging him out from his thoughts.

"Those screams. Do they happen all the time?"

"No," the taller replied. "But the shadow lord is all worked up today about a special opponent that Lord Anton's been sayin' is somethin' special. So I reckon we'll be hearin' nothin' but screams tonight."

Owen gulped. *I suppose that special opponent is me.*

The shouts and jeering of the crowd in the arena began to

intensify, but just as the words became discernible, the three made a turn down a steep flight of stairs. As they passed the second landing, Owen asked, "Where are we going?"

"Beneath the arena. You'll be taken in from there," the shorter responded.

The rest of the way was as bleak as the path before, but at least the shouts were muted. At the end of a long path, Owen saw two other guards dressed similarly to his current companions, standing on either side of an iron-barred door. One of the gatekeepers flicked her head toward them as they approached. "Is this one going in?" she asked.

"Aye, that he is," the taller guard said, his words still as heavy as before.

Nodding, the female guard unlocked the door after checking inside as if ensuring no one might try to rush out. As his companions unlocked his shackles, the taller man made eye contact with Owen once more. The small, half-smile the man gave him conveyed both his wishes of luck and his expression of sorrow. Owen nodded to the man and then stepped into the room beneath the arena.

The iron door screeched as it shut behind him. Its squeal echoed among the stone columns in the circular room. Three men gathered around the single brightly burning brazier in the center of the space. The hands they extended toward the flames were trembling.

Owen cleared his throat and approached. Like him, they'd all been robbed of their clothes and trappings, wearing only trousers and boots.

Do they take our clothing to make us easier targets for the trolls?

Taking a place beside the fire, Owen extended his hands toward the flames. The light and the warmth filled him with a blissful comfort which fueled him like a good meal would a mortal. Sucking in a lungful of the warm air, Owen realized that if he didn't initiate his plan now, he might not be able to.

He tried to make eye contact with any of the men around the brazier, but they already seemed lost. "Have any of you fought up there before?" he started quietly, hoping the guards would not hear him.

One man from across the fire looked up and chuckled. "Lad, those who fight in the arena, die in the arena."

The man on Owen's right gulped.

Nodding, Owen continued, "Listen, I'm a warrior. I've fought demons." The bluff was enough to make the men look at him. "Hear me. Do as I say, and we might all get out of here alive."

The man to his left laughed. "Alive?" He shook his head. "I take it you're still mortal then? *You* listen," the doubter continued. "Our chances were taken from us the second we were stolen from our homes. Look at us. While we were *lucky* enough to be made biters instead of the mindless meals they've made others, we're not fighters. We're farmers and soon to be *dead* farmers at that. Whatever plan you think you've figured out, we'll all be dead within a minute once that troll comes out."

"Leave the troll to me," Owen insisted. He'd never fought a troll, but he had read about them extensively and knew that for all their might, their weakness was in their feet. "Do they give us weapons or anything?"

The man in the middle said, "They leave weapons around the arena for us to use against the troll, but the troll blunders about so much that they're usually smashed ta bits 'fore anyone can make it to them."

Owen nodded. "Please, you must do everything in your power to get as far away from the troll as you can."

"What are you planning?" the doubter asked.

Inhaling deeply, Owen said, "Once the troll is dead, we're expected to kill each other, right?" The majority either held their breath or nodded in reply. "I will kill the troll, but I will not kill any of you. I'll refuse and then, together, we'll all be fighting our way out of here."

All but one of the men in the circle laughed. As their chuckles faded, Owen asked of the man on his right who did not, "What is your name?"

Silence fell around them and the men exchanged glances.

The man swallowed hard, his green eyes locked with Owen's. "Byram. My name is Byram." He stood a little taller as his name passed from his lips.

Owen felt like his chest was going to explode from his happiness. "Byram, I want you to know your sister and mother haven't given up hope. I'm going to do everything I can to get you all back home to the families who love you." Turning to the man in the middle, Owen asked him his name.

"Daniel."

Turning to the last man on his left, the doubter held his chest up high and remained silent until he said, "We're all dead men. What difference does it make if you know our names?"

Owen thought on this a moment then answered, "It's the first step toward giving you back your humanity." His words resonated over the crackles and clacks of the fire. "And together, we're going to fight for your freedom."

CHAPTER 21
THE ARENA

The mechanisms in the wall creaked and clanked. Above the circle of men, the four pieces of the roof above split into large crevices withdrawing into the walls. The floor beneath them shook to life. Owen's heart raced as the platform they stood on began to rise.

"What's happening?" he hollered above the cracklings of the stone around him.

None of the others answered, their eyes locked on what was coming.

Owen looked left and right as the burning brazier cackled as if laughing at the new hell they were approaching. As the platform rose, he saw rows and rows of people staring out at them, some with a demonic glint of excitement in their eyes, many more with fear.

There has to be a thousand of them. He clenched his teeth. *What a fool I was to think our group back at the cabin could take them all on alone.*

To Owen's left, on the far end of the arena, was a large being sitting in an ornate throne.

The shadow lord.

Anton stood just to the demon's left, looking down proudly at Owen.

The platform shook as it leveled with the sand-covered ground of the arena. At the back of the pitch, a rough stone wall stretched from the foot of the ground to the top of the stalactite ceiling, which Owen figured to be as high as the arena was long. On the wall were two gates, a mirror image of the other side beneath the shadow lord's platform.

Except for the crackling fire from dozens of torches, a pressing hush surrounded them. In their dim light, Owen spotted the weapons the men had mentioned. A few spears and short swords leaned against walls so high Owen figured the average man would not be able to scale them.

But could a vampire fly over them? I wonder if any of them have tried before.

The shadow lord raised a white, ashen hand. In the corners of his eyes, Owen could see the men in the arena with him trembling.

Extending his finger and thumb, the demon snapped. The sound reverberated throughout the hall.

The crowds began to shout and jeer across the arena. The sound of chains clanking screamed out. The gates on the far side of the pitch beneath the shadow lord were beginning to part from one another.

And that must be where the troll is kept.

The two men bolted toward the walls at the mid-belt of the arena, rushing for the weapons. Byram stayed beside Owen.

Of course, you're not listening to me and running toward the troll.

Though the doors were more than halfway open, the creature on the other side was still concealed in shadow.

Keeping his eyes locked on the raising iron door, Owen asked Byram, "Can you fly out?"

"I-I think so," Byram's shaking voice responded.

Owen nodded then said, "Wait for my signal then fly off into the crowd. Do whatever it takes to get out of here."

A low, grumble escaped from behind the opening gates.

Owen gulped and the din of the audience lowered.

A hulking figure broke out from the shadows, standing more than three times the height of the tallest men. The creature's bare gray skin amplified the dried blood around its mouthful of bear-like fangs. The troll wore leather armor with spikes sticking out from its short, thick neck all the way down to its meaty ankles.

Its ugly feet and face are exposed though. That has to count for something.

A bear-like roar exploded out from the creature as its beady eyes locked onto the other men now armed with swords. The creature raised fists larger than Owen's head and stormed toward the men.

Owen and Byram ducked behind the blazing fire of the brazier as the troll launched itself across the arena to attack the other men.

The thumping footsteps of the troll beat across the arena. Owen focused on the closed gates as the thunderous roars of the troll drowned out the screams of the other men. The shaking of the earth stopped just as Owen heard the troll's fist swipe through the air. The crowd released a series of oohs.

The screams of the runners stopped.

"Get ready," Owen hissed to Byram. Twenty meters away was the weapon he was going to run for. "Go toward the gates," he motioned to his left, away from the demon and the troll. "And don't stop until you're safe."

Byram nodded and then shut his eyes. He grimaced and

grit his teeth as a pair of black, bat-like wings grew out of his shoulders, ripping his shirt in the process.

The stomps of the troll approached.

To Owen, though the heat of the fire and the pressure made sweat drip from his brow, for the briefest of moments, it felt like time stopped. He could hear his breath, his heartbeat, and, most importantly, he knew his mother was with him.

A calamitous clatter rang out. The troll slapped the brazier from behind them, sending ash and burning logs raining down. The troll roared so loud, Owen clapped his hands over his ears, the piercing sound echoing throughout his body.

Owen looked up. The troll was covered in the blood of his previous companions. It reached its fist high up in the air.

Owen shoved Byram away. "Go!" he screamed.

The troll brought his fist cascading down, but Owen leaped to the right, drawing the troll's attention toward him.

A series of chanting and jeering escaped from the crowd.

Twisting over on the sand, Owen looked back to see the back of Byram's wings disappearing into the sea of people. But now the troll wielded a burning log in his monstrous hand.

Forcing himself from the ground, Owen bolted toward the sword he'd spotted. His boots sank into the sand as he ran, his calves and thighs burning after being locked up in so small a space.

The troll's heavy footfalls thumped behind him.

Owen dove for the sword, his arm outstretched. The troll swiped the burning log, slicing it through the air behind him, missing Owen's back by inches.

Owen's elbow struck the earth, sending waves of pain up through his arm, but his fingers latched around the sword's wooden handle. Spinning over onto his back, Owen lurched back up onto his feet. The screams of the crowd were deafening, but he saw that at least they had not thrown Byram back into the arena.

The troll stopped its charge three meters away and lifted its burning log high into the air. Its tiny, black eyes bore into Owen's.

Almost. Wait for it.

The monster leaned back and the log came slashing down.

Owen leaped forward, driving the sword deep into the top of the troll's gray foot.

As Owen rolled away, the troll roared and dropped to its left knee. Owen ran around the troll with all of his might, crossing the arena toward the other side, his feet sinking deep into the sand.

Don't stop. You have to reach a spear. But where is it? The spear he had spotted earlier was gone. *Stars! Did one of those fools take it?* Owen slid beside the limbs of what was left of a man he'd entered the arena with. His eyes desperately searched the area and the sand for any hint of the weapon he needed.

On the other side of the arena, the troll let out a whine. Owen glanced up. The troll bore the sword in his mighty fist, blood running from his foot. The troll took a step, winced, then hurled the sword at Owen.

Owen ducked, but the brunt of the blade slapped against his shoulders. He felt the troll's warm blood drip down his stinging skin.

Ignoring the pain from the cut on his back, Owen spun his body around to see his opponent. The troll crouched down, settings the knuckles of his balled fists into the sand. His bulbous shoulders framed his snarling, bloodied muzzle.

He's going to charge!

Out of the corner of his eye, Owen spotted something. Peaking out from the sand was the staff of a spear.

On all fours, the troll charged.

Owen dove in the direction of the staff, plunging his hands into the sand. His fingers dug and brushed away the sediment until at last, they found the hard wooden staff. Ripping the pole up, sand raining down, Owen spun around on his knee. The troll was more than halfway across the arena.

Owen raised the spear over his shoulder, extending his left arm out in front of him.

The troll roared.

Owen hurled the spear forward his arm aching with the effort.

The spear corkscrewed through the air, the point shooting into the troll's eye, driving deep into his skull. The monstrous creature went limp and dropped to the earth with a tumultuous thud.

Owen fell to his knees and the crowd went silent.

Through the haze of sand settling in the arena, Owen heard a singular, slow clap. He looked up. Standing from his throne, the demon lord looked down upon him.

CHAPTER 22
THE DEMON

"Well done," the demon's voice hissed.

Owen wiped the sweat from his brow with the back of his hand. Though they were twenty meters apart, Owen could see the demon's eyes glowing red.

"Not only did you kill my troll, you did so without injury, *and* you managed to squeak one of your fellow competitors out. Well done indeed." The demon squared his shoulders and leaned back, his hood falling from his face.

Owen nearly gasped. No natural color touched the skin of the creature before him. The whites of his eyes were nearly the same color of his flesh, which made his red irises all the more bright.

Anton leaned close to the demon and whispered something to him. The demon nodded once then set his hands on the rail separating his throne from the arena. "My companion tells me there's something special about you. I feel it too." The demon's long, clawed fingers rose and fell in waves. "What are you, boy? You are certainly not a wizard, but what else could you be?"

I will never tell you.

Owen stood and slowly approached the center of the arena, never breaking eye contact with the demon. "There's something you should know," Owen started. He motioned toward Anton, "Your second in command, he -"

"He what?" The demon interrupted. A pointed tooth smile radiated out among the demon's white flesh. "He intends to kill me to take my place in hell?"

Anton smirked.

Owen's shoulders dropped.

What is happening?

The demon's cruel chuckle echoed in the hall. Raising his hands, the lord said, "Did you really believe my Anton would betray me? Ha! Behold." He motioned behind Owen.

Spinning around, Owen gasped. Behind him were Helen, Riva and Lann, the iron masks clasped around their necks.

"No," Owen whispered. Any hope of being freed died before his eyes. *Lann can't even change. He can't risk that awful thing strangling him while he tries.*

Though it felt like his heart was lead, Owen turned back to the demon. The monster's cruel laugh echoed throughout the arena.

"Anton just gave you a bit of hope worth fighting for so we might have a good show, and you did not disappoint! Even if Anton had wanted to betray me, I am the lord of shadows, boy!" The demon spat. "Every lie, secret, and sin are *my* dominion. When people try to hide, I see it all. And now, boy." The demon pointed his claw at Owen. "I'll see you."

The demon clasped his fingers. An invisible hand wrapped around Owen's neck, raising him twenty feet into the air, kicking and squirming above the bloodied sand below. Owen's wrists ripped out to the side as if detained by shackles he could not see.

While laughing, the demon raised his other hand. "Let's see your *real* shadow, boy."

Owen's eyes filled with tears. "Please!" he begged through gritted teeth, but his plea fell on deaf ears. Struggle as he did, Owen could not draw his outstretched arms back to his sides.

The demon shot his hand toward Owen.

A jet black carpet ran from the tip of Owen's toes, across the arena floor, past his comrades, and reflected up the stone back of the arena. The shadow's wings extended, its long neck raised, and forced by the demon's spell, its jowls opened wide.

The demon's brows reached high as his deep, belly laugh rang out.

"No!" Lann shouted behind him.

Tears fell down Owen's cheeks. *I'll never be able to go home.*

The demon slapped Anton's shoulder and said, his voice ringing out, "Well done, m' boy, you really did it! A dragon's blood will not only earn our trust in hell...it just might open the gates and bring our king to this plain."

Through the well of tears, Owen shot his gaze to the faces in the crowd. A few looked exuberant, while many more looked appalled.

"Did I not promise you a glorious new beginning?" the demon shouted out to his masses. He whipped his hand back and Owen dropped to the earth.

Owen's side slammed into the sand, the wind knocked from his lungs. Owen rolled over onto his back, clutching onto his stomach. A great commotion erupted from the people in the stands. Through his desperate heaves to regain breath, Owen could not tell if they were cheering or dissenting.

Owen's stinging lungs settled and he drew in a deep, haggard breath. A distinct copper taste filled his mouth.

I'm not just banished from my home. I'm not just going to die here. I'm going to die so that the king of the hell will be released, condemning everything good in this world.

His watering eyes gazed up at the points of stalactites above. From this angle, they almost looked like stars.

The commotion around him faded into silence as a warm, soothing peace settled his soul.

"Get up," a soft voice whispered. "Do what you know is right."

A small smile spread on his lips at his mother's words. He wasn't alone.

Owen rolled to his side. Though his ribs were tender and his shoulder ached, he pushed himself onto his knees. Taking in a deep breath, he looked up to the demon.

The shadow lord's left brow raised as if he was prepared to see a jester's next act instead of a challenge.

"You're right, demon!" Owen flexed his muscles and through gritted teeth, he said, "I am a dragon!"

CHAPTER 23
FIRE, WING, AND STONE

Owen shut his eyes as the power of his blood came to life. His limbs elongated, his tail and neck stretched. His great wings opened.

The slits of his silver eyes locked onto the podium as fire built in his heart.

Anton bolted from the booth, stumbling backward before disappearing into the fleeing masses. Lessers and greaters alike ran from the arena for their lives.

The burning warmth rolled through Owen's throat and burst from his jowls toward the shadow lord. Owen blasted the podium in one continuous blaze. The light brightened the entire arena. From the corners of his eyes, he could see shadows shimmering up the walls, disappearing into every crack and crevice, their shrieks piercing through the roar of his blaze.

Owen continued the blaze until there was no breath left within him. He drew back and shut his mouth, his fangs snapping together.

The wooden pieces of the podium were on fire, many

crumbling to the arena's floor. A blackened, shriveled mass replaced what once had been the demon's ornate throne.

A sharp, white pain radiated from his right side. Owen roared. A hunch-backed Rabeesa had sliced through his scale armor spilling his blood onto the sand. The creature climbed his scales and lapped greedily from the open wound. Owen tried to kick the thing off with his back foot, but a white light shot through the darkness, slapping against the creature and sending it reeling across the arena away from him.

Owen looked back. The guards of his companions had abandoned them and Byram was setting them free. The freed Helen winked at Owen, tapped the end of her wand to her brow, then ran out the gate, disappearing in the darkness.

Stars. I hope you find your sister.

A lightness filled Owen's heart and he turned his horned head back toward the podium. Seeing the black soot and the raining embers, Owen sneered. *And back to hell with -*

The crumpled mass of the throne shifted.

Owen's eyes widened.

The mass began to stand and Owen took a step back.

A clawed hand whipped out from the remains of the throne, casting the burning timber and embers from its form.

It can't be.

The pale body of the demon stood, its clothes burnt, the obese white body almost glowing against the surrounding black. The red, glowing eyes chilled Owen's blood. "And now, Dragon," the shadow lord growled. "*You* will taste the fires of hell!" The demon raised his claws. A ghoulish green orb glowed between its palms.

Owen dug his feet into the sand and felt the fire building from his heart.

The demon's orb blasted toward Owen just as Owen's fire erupted from his jowls. The demon's power radiated against

Owen's blaze. The pair were locked as each tried to blast the other.

How long can he hold this? How long can I?

Every muscle in Owen's body strained, focusing the last of his strength on the might of his fire. The sound of wings rushed by Owen's ear, but he refused to be distracted. His eyes watered and every part of him ached as he struggled to keep billowing. Owen's claws dug into the earth as the air within him waned.

Stars! I'm not strong enough.

In the glow of the demon's light, Owen saw the monster smile, madness beaming in his eyes. He knew he could outlast Owen's blast.

A pair of wings shot through the side of the podium. It happened so fast Owen almost missed seeing Byram's extended arms knocking the demon from its feet.

Owen shut his mouth and drew in a deep breath. "Byram!" his booming voice shouted, unable to distinguish the winged man from the demon as they wrestled one another. His aches forgotten, Owen ran toward the front of the arena, his enormous form crossing it in a few strides.

A clawed hand stomped on Owen's tail, stopping him short. He spun around prepared, to rip apart whatever now challenged him, but his silvery eyes lit up.

Lann's emerald gaze radiated at him between his corkscrew horns.

Owen's heart swelled. *I guess we'll be outcasts together.*

"Draw them apart!" Lann shouted, charging toward the podium.

Owen barreled forward as Byram and the demon rolled over the side of the wall.

The dragons slid to a stop before the wall, sending a wave of sand and dust into the air.

Owen's eyes darted back and forth, straining to see through the dust.

In the cloud, a silhouette began to form, walking toward them.

Owen held his breath and focused on rebuilding the fires within him in case it wasn't Byram emerging.

If it is the demon, can I risk using fire against him if Byram is at his feet?

The sand began to settle and the pale face of the demon emerged. His fanged smile glimmered at them from the darkness. "I am a lord of hell," his voice hissed. "You will *not* extinguish me."

Lann reared back, preparing to blast away, but the memory of how Lann defeated his demon shot into Owen's mind.

He doesn't have scales or armor. He needs his hands to conjure his protection.

Owen whipped around, spinning his tail behind him. Extending his razor-sharp fins, Owen stuck the demon to the sand, pinning him to the earth. Turning to his brother, Owen screamed, "Now!"

A white blast of fire shot from Lann's jowls at the trapped demon. The roar of Lann's blaze was nearly deafening but Owen kept his tail down regardless of the burning heat. Just when Owen thought he'd been burnt to the bone and was about to scream in pain, it stopped.

Lann's scaled chest heaved up and down.

As the dust kicked up from the scorching fires settled, Owen saw that the arena was empty. Not a single shadow, vampire, or mortal had waited around to see what would happen.

Turning his gaze to the end of his tail, Owen's brows shot up. The points of his pronged tail were embedded in glass, but of the demon, there was not a trace.

"How hot did you burn?" Owen asked Lann.

"Apparently, hotter than hell."

Rolling his eyes, Owen pulled his tail out from the glass. The shattered crystals rained upon the sand. Owen took in what felt like his first true breath since he fell into this nightmare, but before he could exhale, a lump lying among the remnants of the podium caught his attention.

"Stars!" Owen rushed to the border of the arena, using the end of his long nose to roll Byram onto his back.

From behind him, he heard his brother hiss a curse.

Byram's eyes were wide and unfocused, staring up to the stalactites above.

Owen dropped his forehead onto Byram's chest. Through his scales, he could feel that Byram was still warm. "If only we were a moment faster," Owen whispered.

Above, soft cracking sounds began to croak to life.

"You hear that?" Lann asked.

Owen looked up. A number of the pointed stalactites above were rocking and quaking.

"We need to get out of here," Lann started. "*Now.*"

"We can't leave him," Owen motioned to Byram.

Lann nodded once then said, "And we cannot make it out as dragons. Hurry up and change so we can carry him out or we're all dead." Lann barely waited to finish his sentence before initiating his transitional spell.

Heeding his brother's words, Owen's bones cracked and his muscles ached as his body shifted. Once his human fingers extended in front of him, he was suddenly so much more aware of how much everything else hurt.

"Help me out, Lann!" Owen demanded as he struggled to shove his arms beneath Byram's limp body.

Lann went around to the other side of Byram and together,

the brothers hoisted him up, pulling his arms around their shoulders.

From above, a sickening crack echoed. Lann and Owen shot their gazes up in time to see a stalactite as tall as a man cascade toward the sand. It spiked into the earth with a thud, reverberating throughout the arena.

Owen gulped.

"Let's move!" Lann shouted, dragging Byram and by extension Owen behind him.

Crack after crack erupted from above as the rain of stone began to hurtle toward the earth.

The brothers ran with all their might toward the other side of the arena, dragging Byram's feet in the sand.

"Look out!" Owen shouted, pulling Byram's body back. The three fell to their backs as an enormous cone slammed into the sand at their feet.

A moan escaped from Byram. As the brothers pulled him to his feet, Owen saw that Byram's eyes were now closed.

Stars! Are you still in there?

"Owen!" Lann shouted, dragging the pair forward.

Owen shook his head and pushed himself forward with the dead weight of Byram on his shoulder.

"Riva!" Lann hollered.

Riva stood in the open gate waving her arms encouraging them to hurry up. "C'mon!" she screamed as her eyes darted to the falling stones above.

A rock the size of a man's head struck Owen's shoulder. White pain shot across his entire body. He screamed, falling to his knees, taking Byram and Lann down with him. Blood gushed down his arm, his human muscle and flesh dangling from his exposed bone.

A pair of hands latched onto Owen and dragged him out of the collapsing cavern into the pathway.

Owen tried to take in a deep breath, but the dust in the tunnel stung his throat and nose. His head began to feel heavier and heavier. He couldn't feel his arm, but he was very aware of the sticky, wet mess running down his side. After blinking hard, Owen saw Riva's lips say *we have to go now* as she wrapped the sleeve she tore from her garment around his arm. Owen's teeth clenched as the fabric tightened over his wound.

He felt Riva help lift his body from the stone floor and push him to move through the passageway. He saw Lann pull Byram from the floor. Owen's heart felt like it was going to erupt from his chest. Byram's eyes were open. He was blinking, his eyes moving.

They heal. He healed!

Though limping, bleeding, and almost broken, the four made their way out through the hells of the passageways, Riva guiding their every step. Loose dirt and rocks fell all around them as the earth beneath their feet rumbled. The walls of the cave trembled as the halls carved from the mountain fell. It seemed as if nature was reclaiming the heart of her mountain from the monsters who'd stolen it from her.

Every step sent daggers radiating through Owen's arm and up through his spine, but he had to keep going.

I have to see the stars again.

"We're almost there!" Riva assured as she dragged them on. "Look! There it is!"

Ahead was an opening to the outside world. The black doors were discarded to the sides as if the fleeing inhabitants of this place had ripped them from their stations and cast them aside.

The four emerged into the night.

We made—the thought died.

A line of torches pointed at them, making Owen's pupils constrict in reaction.

"On your knees!"

A barrage of demands came hurtling at them.

Owen collapsed to the earth, dragging Riva down beside him. He rolled onto his back, relieved he made it out to see the stars, even if he faced death yet again.

CHAPTER 24
AT THE GATES

Though the ground beneath them continued to rumble, the torch-holding guards were unmoved by the commotion.

Lann started to say something, before a familiar voice boomed from behind the line of guards before them, "Let me through!"

Owen looked up, his eyes still adjusting to the brightness. The line of guards parted, allowing one man to split them. "Owen?" the blurred silhouette whispered as he approached. "My sons!" he shouted.

Owen's eyes widened. But before he could say anything, a pair of arms latched around him and pulled him up from the ground. He took a deep breath, letting the familiar scents of his father bring him home.

Lann slammed into the pair of them, joining the embrace. While his family held tight to him, Owen tried to ignore the sickening pain emanating from his arm. His vision had settled and he could make out the details of the ten figures, their fellow dragons, accompanying his father. Owen's heart twisted. At first, he was so grateful to see his kin he thought he might cry, but then he noticed the melancholy expressions on the two elders.

Oh no. They know.

Sten pushed his boys back and threw his own fur coat over Owen's bare shoulders. "Oh, my sons. It seems you had quite a bit more than just a scouting mission, hmm?"

The brothers nodded, both too exhausted to say anything.

Motioning to a group of people standing near the edge of the road winding down the mountain, Sten said, "Your friend filled us in on what happened, well, parts of it at least."

Our friend?

Owen narrowed his focus and saw Helen standing rigid, her eyes pointed straight to the earth. He heard his father say, "She said two *dragons* saved them all from the demon." However, Owen did not stay to hear the rest of what his father had to say. He gently pushed away from his family, limping down the slight grade to join Helen's side. The torn flesh in his arm stung and itched like mad as it healed itself, but none of that mattered to Owen. He had to know what happened to Helen's sister.

"Helen?" he softly called.

Seeing her trembling, he softly took a hold of her hand.

She jumped, pointing her wand to his face.

"Easy," he cooed, stroking the top of her hand with his thumb.

Her eyes searched him, then she leaned into his arms and began to sob. Owen's heart broke. He knew without her saying anything that her sister did not make it. Cradling the back of her head to his chest, Owen looked up at the two dozen or so survivors who accompanied her. They were all strangers to him, but unlike the others, they stayed. Anton and those like him were gone.

They must've just missed the dragons. Stars, what'll become of this lot? After all they've been through, can they ever go home again?

Helen continued to weep into his chest until Riva joined their sides. "Owen," she called quietly. He drew his gaze to hers. A grimacing Byram joined her side

I bet he's aching like I am.

Riva swallowed hard then said, "Your father would like a word, Owen."

Nodding, Owen gently pushed Helen back. He held on to her shoulders then said, "I'll be right back, alright?"

She snuffled then nodded.

As he turned, Owen saw Riva take hold of Helen, letting her tears fall on her shoulder.

With Helen's soft sobs behind his back, Owen approached the elders standing with his father. Lann passed him, sucking his lips so tightly Owen thought they might burst. Lann nodded to him as they passed as if trying to assure him that everything would be alright.

How can it be? Because of my stupidity, I've stolen our home from you too.

Before he joined the elders, he sent one last look up at the sheet of stars above.

The torch bearers took a few more steps away from the elders, granting them enough light while maintaining their privacy.

"Owen," Varden's deep voice started. He sent a sideways look to Airell who appeared to be fighting back tears. "While you and your brother removed a great evil from this world, you both broke your vows of concealing your birth rites from mortals."

Owen shot his gaze to the ground. While his arm had

almost completely healed, his shoulders now felt as heavy as stone.

"I'm so sorry, m' boy," Varden continued. "Because of this, neither of you will be allowed to come home."

"I understand," Owen said, his lips barely opening enough to let the words pass.

"Varden," Sten started. "Are you *absolutely* certain there is no other way?"

Varden shook his head, "They broke the oath. I know their hearts were in the right place, but they've endangered us all. The demons will never stop hunting him and his brother. Stars know what the vampires who got away will do." Varden rubbed his brows. "For the safety of our kin, they cannot come home, Sten."

Sten moved to speak, but Owen interrupted, "It's alright, Father." Looking back to Lann, Riva, Byram, and Helen, Owen smiled. "Truth be told, my mission's not over yet. The demon's right hand, Anton, got away. I suspect he's not going to just give up his desire for power, so easily." Owen shrugged. "I think I've found a team that'll help me find him and stop him."

Airell pressed her hands to her cheeks.

Varden dipped his brow to Owen then turned away to join the other dragons.

Airell took a step toward Owen and said, "We're always just a smoke signal away. Don't forget that, alright?" She winked then also returned to the sides of their brothers and sisters.

"Owen," Sten's shoulders dropped. "I'm so sorry, I can keep talking to them to see if -"

"Father," Owen held up his hands. His left arm was still sore, but the traces of his injury were almost all healed. "I'll be alright. I've got Lann, after all. I wouldn't have made it far without him. Wouldn't be standing here at all without him."

Sten pulled his son into his arms once more and held him tight. "I want you to know your mother and I are both so proud of you." Owen felt his heart swell. "You did what was right no matter the cost."

Tears ran from Owen's eyes.

"I love you, Son," Sten said. "And like Airell said, we're never too far away."

Owen bit his lower lip. "I love you too." He leaned away and glanced back at his group. "These mates we've made, I don't know how or what yet, but something in my gut is telling me that destiny has something big in store for us."

Sten chuckled. "You're your mother's boy, alright." He placed his hand on Owen's cheek then said, "Follow your gut and never forget that if you feel lost, look to the stars. Now go. Go make this world a better place together."

Returning to his companions, Owen once more pulled Helen to his side. Her puffy eyes looked up and the hope he saw glimmering back at him convinced him this was the right decision.

"So...dragons, eh?" Riva asked with a tilt of her head. "Didn't see that coming."

"*Banished* dragons," Lann corrected, his voice heavy. He lifted his shoulders then said, "But it sure seems like we have enough here to keep us occupied."

Standing up straighter than she had since they'd emerged from the cave, Helen said, "We *have* to find Anton."

Riva pointed to the vampire refugees. "We also have to find a home for all of them."

Owen motioned toward Byram then added, "*And* we have to get you home to your mother and sister. Well, after thanking you a thousand times over for saving all of us."

Byram shrugged. "Consider us even."

Owen sent one last look back to the dragons as his fellows

began their descent down the mountain. He knew they would ebb off from one another as they neared the base, disappearing off into the woods before transforming and heading back for their home.

"Then what?" Riva asked, splitting the silence. "I don't see the five of us really settling in after all of this."

Everyone in their circle turned their gaze to Owen. The trust in their eyes was as inspiring to him as the stars above. Owen drew in a deep breath and the words poured from his lips, "We go to the house of Dova. Helen said they're training people there to standardize magic. We train people in how to fight demons or find a way to ensure the gates never open for the king of the damned."

Lann nodded and said, "Sounds like a plan."

The five rounded up their refugees and began the trek down the mountain toward the cabin. They had many challenges ahead to build a brighter tomorrow, but they would do it together.

ACKNOWLEDGMENTS

I wanted a teaser chapter, not quite a prologue and certainly not a full novel, introducing *The Blue Dragon Society* series, which, at the time, had been in my mind for over twenty years. In a totally unrelated conversation, my business partner, Theresa Halvorsen, and I were joking about the shape-shifting fad in new releases. I think we had just seen a cover of a blue alien-werewolf man and that led her to mention shapeshifting dragons. To say an idea was sparked is an extreme exaggeration. What had eluded me for years, was solved in a moment; the origin story of how the Blue Dragon Society was formed.

Similarly, I'd always wanted to somehow incorporate my origin story explaining vampires in this series, but I never knew how. I'd always thought it'd be a neat idea to have vampires be the product of a deal with the devil in their attempt to escape plague. Anton, my deliciously vicious villain was born on the page in the first draft of this story. He'd never presented himself to me before and neither had any of the other characters in this story, with the exception of Byram, who has many parts yet to play.

I knew I wanted to write a story about brothers, but otherwise, those were all the pieces I had. The bones of my story were forged, but it had a lot of growing pains. It took about two and a half months to write my first draft and another couple of months of editing and read throughs. During this time, major life changes were occurring for me. No Bad Books Press was preparing for our first appearance as vendors at Comic-Con. I was struggling to establish myself as a full time author, I'd quit my full-time job to pursue writing, which sounds amazing, but it totally flipped my writing habit. I had to change my twelve-year writing habit from writing before I fell asleep to writing in the morning, something I had never done, and while it doesn't sound like much, it was a big change for me and I struggled for a long while. On top of all that, my child, my cat, fell very ill and was diagnosed with cancer. It felt like I'd been struck in the heart. It hadn't been a year since our other cat, Lil Kitty was lost to cancer, so I fell into depression. Writing became my medicine once more, my way to escape. I forced myself to write the first draft and even the second, but after my rounds of edits with Theresa and another friend, my creative juices kicked back into gear and this "short story" turned into the novella (or "short novel" depending on who you ask) you now hold. While writing *Origins* felt like pulling teeth at times, I am so grateful for this story. It has helped to fill in holes that plagued the rest of the series.

The original story and dialogue had actually been much more adult, but after chatting with the author of the Murphy's Law series, K.A. Fox about how her books are accessible to young adults, I decided to soften some elements, making this book much more available to a wider audience range. My niece and nephew had been asking me for YEARS to write a novel that they could read and this seemed like the perfect opportunity. The rest of *The Blue Dragon Society* series will be adult, but there was something about this tale that felt right being written so that thirteen year olds could talk about it with their parents.

A tremendous thank you to Theresa Halvorsen who is a

dear friend and has perpetually helped my writing to grow. To my darling Salvatore, thank you for always believing in me. To Victoria, to Kori, to Jenny, thank you always for all the laughter. And to my cat assistant, Bella Tuna Todd, I would be lost without you.

ABOUT THE AUTHOR

S. Faxon is a creative warrior. On top of writing dark fantasy, horror, and thriller novels, she is a speculative fiction cover designer. She is a member of the Horror Writers Association, the Independent Book Publishers Association, San Diego Writers, Ink, and the San Diego Writers and Editors Guild. Sarah also co-stars in the writing podcast, Semi-Sages of the Pages and she is the co-founder of the hybrid press, No Bad Books Press, with her business partner, Theresa Halvorsen.

She loves the sound of rain and the scent of ink on legal pads. Sarah lives in San Diego and creates under the careful eye of her cat assistant, Bella Tuna Todd.

To stay up to date on S. Faxon's creative projects, follow her on Goodreads and sign up to receive insights from her weekly newsletter on her website, sfaxon.com.

ALSO BY S. FAXON

The Animal Court

Foreign & Domestic Affairs

Tiny Dreadfuls

Lost Aboard

Released

Made in the USA
Las Vegas, NV
20 March 2022

46027002R00100